# HIS ONE WISH . . .

"Ready or not, here I come," Michael whispered. He launched himself at Kyle, running full out. He lowered his shoulder and rammed Kyle to the ground before rat boy even had a chance to turn around.

Michael grabbed both of Kyle's wrists and pinned them behind his back.

"You just keep eating pavement until we're finished with our little chat. You got that, Kyle?" Michael demanded. He jabbed his knee into the loser's back, just to make his point clear.

"I'm not Kyle," the guy said, his words muffled against the asphalt of the parking lot.

"What?" Michael grabbed the guy by the shoulders and flipped him over.

He wasn't lying. He definitely wasn't Kyle. This guy looked more like Michael than he did like Kyle.

For a long moment the stranger just looked at him in silence, causing Michael's adrenaline to start pumping all over again. What did this guy *want*?

"I'm your brother," he finally said.

Don't miss any books in this fascinating
new series from Pocket Books

# ROSWELL
## HIGH

**#1 The Outsider**
**#2 The Wild One**
**#3 The Seeker**
**#4 The Watcher**
**#5 The Intruder**
**#6 The Stowaway**
**#7 The Vanished**
**#8 The Rebel**

All Pocket Books are available by post from:
**Simon & Schuster Cash Sales**. PO Box 29
Douglas, Isle of Man IM99 1BQ
Credit cards accepted.
Please telephone 01624 836000
fax 01624 670923, Internet
http://www.bookpost.co.uk or email:
bookshop@enterprise.net for details

# ROSWELL
## HIGH

# THE REBEL

by

MELINDA METZ

POCKET
BOOKS

This book is a work of fiction. Although the physical setting of the book is Roswell, New Mexico, the high school and its students, names, characters, places and incidents are either products of the author's imagination or are used fictitiously. Any resemblance to actual events or locales or persons, living or dead, is entirely coincidental.

An imprint of Simon & Schuster UK Ltd. A Viacom Company
Africa House, 64-78 Kingsway, London WC2B 6AH

Produced by 17th Street Productions,
an Alloy Online, Inc. company
33 West 17th Street, New York, NY 10011

A CIP catalogue record for this book is available from the British Library

ISBN 07434 0890X

1  3  5  7  9  10  8  6  4  2

Printed by Omnia Books Ltd, Glasgow
First published in USA in 1998 by Archway Paperbacks.

# ONE

Max Evans spread a thin layer of spicy brown mustard over his AstroNut bar, careful not to miss a spot. This would be the first time the beings of his home planet tasted the candy, and he wanted the experience to be perfect. He raised the AstroNut bar to his nose and took a long, deep sniff. The scent of the mustard made the inside of his nose tingle, and the hint of chocolate and coconut started the saliva pumping in his mouth.

He smiled as he felt the impatience of the beings who made up the collective consciousness grow. He waited another moment until they were practically begging for it, then he took the first bite. The flavors exploded in his mouth—the salt of the somewhat stale peanuts, the overwhelming exotic sweetness of the coconut, the slight bitterness of the dark chocolate.

Max had probably eaten more than a thousand AstroNuts in his life, but now, with the reactions of the beings of the consciousness ripping through him, it was like he was tasting the candy for the first time. And he was aware of so much more than simply flavor. Like the way the chocolate felt against his tongue, smooth and cool. And the way the nuts crunched under his teeth. And the way the mustard traced a line of heat down his throat.

"Can I have a bite?" Maria DeLuca asked.

It took Max a second to register the question because he was so absorbed in the response of the consciousness, he'd pretty much forgotten he was sitting in the school cafeteria with Maria, Liz Ortecho, Michael Guerin, and Max's sister, Isabel. Every day the connection between him and the beings grew stronger, so much so that he sometimes spaced on where he was and who he was with.

"Come on, Max. I'll love you forever," Maria begged. She twined one of her bouncy blond curls around her finger.

Max grinned at her. You just had to grin at Maria when she went into full-out cute mode.

"Hey, back off, *chiquita*. That's *my* man you're talking to," Liz mock threatened, her dark brown eyes narrowing.

"Well, tell *your* man to share his candy bar with *your* best friend," Maria shot back.

"Take it," Max said, reaching across the cafeteria table and holding the AstroNut bar in front of Maria's mouth so that she could take a bite. "I don't want to cause a catfight," he added with a smirk.

Michael slapped his hands over Maria's lips an instant before the candy brushed against them. "I'm not letting you do this," he told her. "Clearly you're suffering from some kind of temporary insanity. How long has it been since you allowed a preservative to enter the 'temple that is your body,' as you insist on calling it?"

"Besides, it will give you zits," Isabel added.

"But Max doesn't have any," Maria protested, the words coming out muffled by Michael's fingers.

"Yeah, that's because Max spends half an hour in front of the mirror every morning using his power to clear up his face," Isabel answered. She flipped her long blond hair over her shoulder.

"Hey, some things are supposed to remain private," Max told his sister.

Maria wriggled out of Michael's grasp, grabbed the candy bar from Max, and took a huge bite.

"So, what'd you think?" Max asked her once she'd chewed and swallowed.

She wrinkled her nose. "I can't believe we were eating the same thing," she answered. She lowered her voice. "I mean, I know aliens have different taste buds or whatever, but I saw your face. You looked like you were about to have an or—" She stopped midsentence, and her cheeks got all pink.

"A what?" Michael pressed, his gray eyes flashing with amusement. "Come on, Maria, a what?"

"A . . . a . . . an original experience," she blurted out, her cheeks going from pink to near purple.

"Now that I'm connected to the consciousness, it's

like everything is new to me," Max explained. "When I tasted the AstroNut, it wasn't just me, it was all these beings who'd never had anything like it."

"Can't you just block them out?" Isabel asked.

"I used to decide when I wanted to make the connection," Max explained. "Now it's pretty much permanent, but I can sort of turn the volume up or down."

"Permanent," Isabel repeated. She stacked her empty sweetener packets, making sure all the edges were perfectly in line, then she reached across the table, snagged Liz's empty sugar packet, and stuck it on the top of the pile.

She's freaked by the idea, Max realized. Isabel always went into her clean-and-organize routine when she was upset.

"It's actually kind of cool," he told her. "It's like everything you do, you're doing it for the first time. Their reactions feel almost like your reactions, and everything becomes much more . . . intense."

"But you can't turn them off. You can only turn them down. Is that the deal?" Michael asked. He didn't sound happy.

"Pretty much," Max answered.

Michael shoved his hands through his spiky black hair. "I read about this guy in Japan who agreed to stay in his apartment for one year and have his whole life broadcast on TV. He only got to have stuff he won in contests, so at first he didn't have food, or clothes, or even toilet paper. The guy was wiping his butt

4

with his hand, and everyone was watching him on the tube." Michael paused for breath and jabbed his finger at Max. "You're that guy, Max."

"Hey, I always use toilet paper," Max joked.

Michael didn't even crack a smile. "Pretty soon I'm going to be that guy, too."

"Even I'm going to be that guy," Isabel said.

It was true, or at least it was true that Michael and Isabel would have to make their own connections to the consciousness when they went through their *akinos*. If they didn't, they'd die.

"And anyway, you're the one who's going to have most of the *original experiences*," Michael said. "If I eat an AstroNut after my *akino,* the consciousness will have already tasted it through you, so—"

"Forget the chocolate bar," Isabel interrupted. "Max, if you're going to insist on being in communication with the beings, at least talk about something important," she snapped. "Have you even bothered to ask them about Alex today?"

A wave of guilt crashed over Max. Alex Manes was one of his best friends. It hadn't even been two weeks since Alex had gotten sucked through the wormhole and ended up on Max's home planet.

"I'll do it right now," Max answered. He took a couple of slow breaths and allowed his connection to the beings to deepen until he felt his aura begin to dissolve into the ocean of auras that formed the consciousness.

He formed a mental picture of Alex—dark red hair, green eyes—trying to mix in a sense of Alex's wacked sense of humor and his take-no-prisoners attitude when it came to protecting the people he cared about. Then he threw the image out into the consciousness and surfed through the auras, picking up their reactions.

What he got back reassured him. Alex was alive, unharmed. The beings were still getting used to his presence, but they—

Suddenly Max hit a pocket of auras that felt like molten steel. He'd been swept into this pocket before—or another one just like it. The beings here feared Alex, and their fear produced a hatred so strong that it seared Max's skin. These beings couldn't tolerate Alex on their planet. They wanted to kill him.

The living fire shot into Max's nose and throat and ears. When the three streams met—an explosion detonated inside him. He could almost feel his organs roasting.

He couldn't survive this. His body was going to combust. His—

A hand shook Max's shoulder hard, and he shoved himself away from the consciousness—as far away as the connection allowed. His eyes refocused on the cafeteria, and he saw Liz staring at him, her lips tight with concern.

"Are you all right?" she demanded, loosening

her grip. "You looked like you were having a night-mare or something."

Max shoved his blond hair off his forehead. He stared down at the skin of his hands and arms. Completely undamaged. Not even a tinge of red-ness. "I'm okay."

"And Alex?" Michael asked.

"He's okay, too," Max reassured them. There was nothing the others could do to stop the beings if they moved against Alex. Max promised himself to keep his connection to the consciousness as tight as possible. That way he'd feel if something started to go down, and he could try to intervene . . . somehow. "Most of the beings have accepted Alex's presence."

"But is our home planet a democracy?" Isabel muttered.

"We can't risk it. We've got to work up another plan to get Alex back," Liz said.

"A plan? Gee, what a great idea," Michael shot back sarcastically. "Let's recap for the viewers who tuned in late. The only power source strong enough to give us a shot at getting Alex back is the Stone of Midnight. Elsevan DuPris, alien psy-chopath and the killer of my true parents and Isabel and Max's and Adam's, has the Stone."

Isabel took the pepper shaker off her stack of empty packets. She reshuffled them—sweetener packet, sweetener packet, sugar packet, sweetener packet—then put the shaker back in place.

Michael kept talking. Max wished he would shut up, but he knew Michael well enough to be sure that wasn't going to happen.

"Oh yeah, and we have no idea where DuPris is," Michael ranted, his eyes locked on Liz, who was meeting his gaze straight on, "and since he can take on the appearance of anyone he wants, he could be sitting at the next table, getting ready to assassinate us all, and we wouldn't have a clue. He could also be in Africa or on some other planet."

"He could even be in Canada," Maria joked. She glanced from Max to Liz to Isabel to Michael, clearly hoping one of them would laugh. Max tried and gave something that sounded more like a cough.

"And oh yeah," Michael rushed on. "DuPris also has the ship, so we can't even attempt to try and figure out how to use it to go after Alex." Neither he nor Liz blinked, both seeming determined to win their battle of the stares. "All caught up now?"

"Yeah, Michael. Thanks," Liz answered. "I don't know what we'd do if I didn't have you around to explain things. You're so much smarter than every-one else."

"Don't fight, you guys," Maria begged. She wrapped her fingers around Michael's arm, then reached across the table and grabbed Liz's hand. "If you do, I'll have to come up with more lame jokes. Even worse than the Canada attempt."

Max was glad Maria had jumped in. Sometimes he got sick of always being the peacemaker of the group.

"Sorry, Liz. I just—," Michael began.

"I know. Bygones," Liz answered, her brown eyes turning warm again.

"Can't you explain to the beings that it's not Alex's fault that he's there?" Isabel asked.

"I have. A bunch of times," Max told her.

"Well, do it again!" Isabel exclaimed. She swept her little pile of wrappers and the pepper shaker onto the floor.

She was obviously way more upset than Max had realized. "Okay, okay," he said.

He closed his eyes and felt his consciousness, his individuality, get loose and slippery. He let himself slide back into the ocean of beings.

There was something different. The ocean felt cooler, and each time Max's aura touched one of the others, a tingling sensation skittered through him.

It's power, he realized. Power building. A lot of power.

He sent out a wave of confusion and waited for one of the beings to send back an explanation. It didn't come.

The tingling grew to an electric sizzle. The auras around him grew brighter, glowing with an oily phosphorescence. Max's own aura turned from emerald to luminous acid green.

What is—

Before Max could complete the thought, a blast of supercharged power blew him out of the ocean. He hurtled away from the other auras, his being vibrating with the shock until it felt like he would fly apart, heading off in every direction.

He felt his molecules shudder and begin to separate. His vision dimmed. His heart fluttered in his chest. What . . . what . . . what—

His mind wasn't functioning properly. The molecules of his brain were too far apart. He couldn't . . . couldn't . . .

"Max, come back! Come back!" Liz cried.

He felt something cool and wet on his face. He jerked open his eyes and saw Maria leaning across the table, wiping a wet napkin over his forehead.

"Now what happened?" Michael demanded. He was gripping the edge of the cafeteria table with both hands, his fingers almost white with the strain.

Max took the napkin from Maria and scrubbed his face hard. "I don't know," he finally admitted. "There was a massive explosion of power in the consciousness, and I got basically thrown free."

"Is Alex all right?" Isabel exclaimed. "Did *whatever*, did it hurt him? Did it kill—"

"I don't know," Max repeated. He felt like some of his neurons were tangled or something. He could feel faint tendrils of shock and grief and pain from the beings, but nothing more.

"So, um, who wants to go with me to my little brother's basketball game after school?" Maria piped up. She gave a short jerk to the left with her chin, and Max saw Kyle Valenti striding up to them.

Kyle Valenti. Son of the late Sheriff Valenti, the man Max and the others had thought was their most dangerous enemy. Until they met DuPris. The very much still alive DuPris.

"So who wants to go?" Maria repeated, her voice edged with a manic cheerfulness.

"I'll go," Michael said. His tone was casual, but Max could see the tension in Michael's body. "Where is it?"

"At the Y," Maria answered. She picked up a baby carrot and stuck the whole thing in her mouth. It looked like she'd suddenly forgotten how to chew. Or like she'd forgotten that's even what you did after you put food in your mouth.

Kyle sat down next to Liz without saying a word. He slammed a stack of photos on the table.

Isabel fanned out the photos, and Max ran his eyes across them. He saw Isabel, Michael, Maria, Alex, Liz, and himself. In various combinations. In various locations. They'd been taken over a period of months, Max realized. Someone had been tracking him and his friends.

Max struggled to keep his face expressionless. He didn't want Kyle to have the satisfaction of any kind of reaction.

"My father took these," Kyle announced, saying each word slowly and deliberately. "He had you under observation. I want to know why. And I want to know where he is. And I want to know now."

For one wild moment Max thought about telling Kyle the truth. It's not like he'd believe it. Max tried to imagine it: See, Kyle, your dad was an agent with an organization called Project Clean Slate, whose mission was to track down aliens on earth, experiment on them, and possibly exterminate them. Somebody in Clean Slate, though not your dad, since he wasn't old enough, found one alien in an incubation pod left on earth after the Roswell Incident—you know, where that spaceship crashed out in the desert in the forties.

Oh, and just FYI, so you have the whole story, Michael, Isabel, and I were in pods just like it, but Clean Slate didn't find us.

Anyway, when the alien in the pod Clean Slate found finally completed the maturation process and broke free more than forty years later, your dad locked it in a secret underground compound. You following me, Kyle? He called the alien Adam, and, oh yeah, he had Adam call him Dad. So I guess that makes Adam like your brother or something.

Anyway, this *other* alien, DuPris, the big enchilada of aliens, the alien who caused the ship to crash in the first place, he took control of Adam and used Adam to kill your dad. Yeah, Adam, well, really DuPris, blasted him with enough power to turn him into a pile of ashes on the floor. Anything else I can help you with?

Yep. That would go over *real* well.

Michael picked up one of the pictures. Max leaned over to get a look. It showed Michael and Maria sprawling on Michael's bed at his last foster home, in the middle of a serious kiss. Valenti had to have been practically right outside the window when he took it, or else he had a state-of-the-art telephoto lens.

Max shot a glance at Maria. She'd finally started chewing her carrot. He could see that she was trying to act totally normal—they all were. But the loose sleeves of her poet's shirt were fluttering, and it was totally clear that Maria was trembling.

"I don't think you should show these to people," Michael told Kyle, giving up the attempt to hide his fury. He slapped the photo facedown on the table. "Unless you want everyone to know your dad was a perv."

Kyle locked eyes with Michael. Max frantically tried to figure out what to do in order to get one of them to back down.

Then the bell rang.

Kyle shoved himself to his feet and swept up the photos. "This isn't over," he warned them. "Sooner or later, I'm getting the truth about what happened to my father. And I'm getting it from one of you."

\*　　\*　　\*

"Go, Kevin!" Maria leaped to her feet. "Go, go, go!"

Michael reached out, snagged her by the elbow, and pulled her back down to her seat next to him on the bleachers. "That is a ten-year-old boy out there on the court," he explained. "What you just did qualifies as cruel and unusual punishment."

Maria smiled at him. "I know. But my mom and dad aren't here to humiliate him—since the big D they try never to be at the same place at the same time—so I have to do it," she explained. "I mean, isn't complaining about your family's behavior key to ten-year-old male bonding?"

"I guess," Michael mumbled. Like he was supposed to know? Well, maybe he should. He'd had more families than pretty much any kid. Foster families, anyway. He should be in *The Guinness Book of World Records*.

He suddenly got the feeling that he was being watched. Oh yeah, he told himself. Everybody is staring at the pathetic boy who doesn't have a family. They're all about to burst into tears over your hard, hard life.

"Oh, I'm so stupid. How could I have asked you about fam—you don't have a—" Maria turned to the mom type sitting next to her. "Can you give me a hand?" she asked. "My foot is stuck so far down my throat, I don't think I'll be able to get it out by myself."

"I know the feeling," the woman answered. Then she jumped up. "Great job, Robbie!" she shouted, punching her fist in the air.

"Don't sweat it," Michael told Maria. "It's not like I need a family. Not now that I have my own place."

He still could hardly believe that Ray Iburg, the only adult survivor of the crash besides DuPris, had left him the UFO museum and the apartment above it. Free at last. Oh, baby, he was free at last.

"But a family isn't just—," Maria began. Then she stopped herself.

"I have you and everyone else for the other stuff," Michael answered. He couldn't quite believe he'd actually said that out loud. But it was true. They were his family in every way that mattered.

Maria gave his hand a quick squeeze, then let it go fast. "I guess that means I have to humiliate you, too, then, huh?" she asked. "Come on, do a wave with me."

"You can't do a wave with two people," Michael answered.

"Just because it's never been attempted before doesn't mean it can't be done," Maria insisted. And Michael knew that in another minute he'd be jumping up with his hands over his head. When you were with Maria, some things were just inevitable.

Like that time she'd made him help her decorate a cake. Not just watch. Help.

He was struck by a flash of memory—him licking a glob of icing off Maria's finger. A jolt of heat zigzagged through him as he thought about it. Don't even go there, he ordered himself. He and Maria were finally getting to be friends again. Real friends. There was no way Michael was going to mess things up by even getting close to that line between friendship and the kind of thing Valenti had immortalized in that picture.

Yeah, it would feel good to kiss Maria again. It would feel amazing. And his body wanted it, no question. But his mind, or his heart, or whatever knew that there was still a girl called Cameron out there. And that—

"Okay, if Kevin's team makes this basket, we do it," Maria told him, yanking him out of his thoughts. "You first, then me."

Michael watched as the kid with the ball hurled it toward the basket. It bounced from the backboard to the rim, teetered, then *swish*.

"Whoo-hoo!" Michael shouted as he jumped to his feet and swept his arms up and down. He figured if he was going to do it, he should *do* it.

Maria jumped up next, going all the way up on her toes as she thrust her arms into the air. Michael tried very hard not to notice the expanse of creamy, soft-looking skin bared by her hiked-up sweater.

He forced his eyes back to the game, then got that feeling again. That prickly feeling of being watched. Of course you're being watched, you big idiot, he told himself. You just did a two-person wave.

A kid with a crew cut grabbed the ball from one of Kevin's teammates. He took off for the other side of the court. The ref blew the whistle and rolled his hands around each other.

"No way!" a man in a suit yelled from the opposite bleachers. "Cameron's never gotten called for traveling!"

Michael felt Maria stiffen, just slightly, but enough for him to notice. He thought, at least he'd wanted to think, that Maria was over the Cameron situation.

But she'd really laid herself on the line when she'd told him that he had to choose between her and Isabel. She'd made herself—what was that chick word?—*vulnerable*. And he'd all but shoved it in her face that he wasn't choosing anyone but Cameron. Cameron, who then left without even bothering to wake him up and say good-bye.

Michael shot a quick glance at Maria. She was watching the game, seemed okay. If he hadn't caught that little reaction when that man had shouted out, "Cameron," he wouldn't even know she'd been bothered by it.

It's not like Maria and I were a couple, he thought. It's not like I dumped her for Cameron.

But he'd known that Maria loved him. She'd told him that before he even met Cameron. Maria had guts that way. She would tell people how she felt even if she wasn't sure she'd like what she heard back from them.

"Want to do another wave?" he asked her. He wanted to do *something* to show her that she was important to him. A wave was probably an exceedingly dorky way to do it, but hey, this was Maria. Dorky things made her happy.

"Not now. The other team's about to score," she answered. At least she looked at him when she said it, looked at him and smiled one of her Maria smiles. "Besides," she added. "People are still staring at us from the last one."

So she felt it, too.

Michael did a quick scan of the people sitting around them. Everyone was watching the kids play, except one older-sister type who was surreptitiously reading a book.

But he still couldn't shake the feeling of being watched. In fact, the feeling was getting stronger.

Michael did a sweep of the opposite bleachers, methodically glancing from face to face. His muscles instinctively tensed when he got to a pair of eyes drilling directly into his.

Kyle Valenti was giving him the death stare. Which Michael couldn't care less about. Even if Michael didn't have powers, he could take on Kyle.

But the hair on the back of his neck stood up when Kyle moved his gaze from Michael to Maria. Maria didn't have any powers. She didn't have any way to defend herself against Kyle.

Michael slid a little closer to Maria. He wasn't going to let anything happen to her. If Kyle took one step toward Maria—one step—Michael would take him out. Permanently.

# TWO

Liz and Max sat on the sofa in the Evanses' living room. Key word: *sat.* Liz tried to remember if there'd ever been a time where they'd been alone in his house and just . . . sat.

Okay, Max wasn't a guy who attacked one second after they found a semiprivate place. But when Liz was alone with Max, the air just got sort of charged. Liz loved that pre-make-out time, where she became more and more aware of everything. The heat that she could feel coming off Max's body. The tickle of her long hair against her back. The sound of Max's breathing getting just subtly faster. The feeling of her own breath easing in and out of her lungs. It felt almost like they were touching each other even before they started touching.

But now . . . they were definitely just sitting. The air didn't feel charged. It smelled stale and felt almost too thick and heavy to breathe.

I'm going to suffocate if I stay in here too long, Liz thought wildly. Then she told herself she was being idiotic. The air had just as much oxygen as it always did.

Liz shot a glance at Max. She wondered if he was aware that she was in the room with him. Or if he was aware that *he* was in the room. She doubted it. He had that look he always got when he was in deep communion with the consciousness. Liz hated that look—all vacant and deanimated. It was like Max wasn't Max anymore. The *thing* sitting next to her was shaped like Max, but it was totally lifeless.

I could slide my hand up his thigh right now, and he probably wouldn't even twitch, Liz thought.

And the worst part was that Max liked connecting to the consciousness. He liked being part of something so immense. He didn't seem to realize that submerging himself in the ocean of beings meant being away from her. Or if he did realize it, he didn't care.

Liz tucked one leg under herself. Then she twisted around and sat cross-legged. She just couldn't get comfortable. She tried a pillow behind her back. Didn't help. She tossed the pillow over onto the armchair.

I have to get out of here, she thought. If I stay here another minute, I'm going to start screaming and never stop.

"Max," Liz said loudly. "Want to head over to the Y? We can still catch part of Kevin's game."

He didn't answer. She leaned over, braced her forefinger against her thumb, then flicked him on the head. He blinked twice.

"The creature stirs," Liz muttered.

"Sorry. Did you say something?" Max asked. He rubbed his temple, right over the place she'd just flicked. Poor baby, Liz thought. Even in her head it came out sounding sarcastic.

"I asked if you wanted to swing by the Y, hang out with Maria and Michael," she said.

"Actually, I'm not feeling that great," Max admitted. "I don't know what's going on in the consciousness, but it's something mega. I keep getting hit with all this fear and anger and, I don't know, sadness, I guess."

"Is it about Alex?" Liz demanded.

"It's something new. I know that. Maybe it could be connected to Alex, but I don't think so." Max shook his head, the movement making him wince.

Liz felt a lance of guilt stab into her. She'd been so caught up in whining to herself about how Max wasn't paying any attention to *her* that she hadn't noticed what was going on with *him*. Now that she was really looking at him, she could see the signs she should have caught before—the purple smudges under his eyes, the way the skin of his forehead appeared somehow tight, the tense muscles in his neck.

"Want me to rub your shoulders?" Liz offered. "My papa always does that for Mama when she gets all stressed, trying to fill too many cake orders in one day."

"Um, actually, I think if you touch me, it's only

going to make it worse," Max said. He gave her an apologetic smile. "I feel like even a feather brushing against me would be killer right now."

Liz nodded. "How about some ice water? Or could I get you a pillow or something?"

"You know what?" Max said. "Why don't you head out? I think I'm just going to try and sit very still until this goes away."

Going out into the fresh air sounded wonderful. Going over to the Y and hanging out with some people who might actually laugh and talk and everything sounded even better. But she wasn't sure Max should be alone.

"I could sit with you," Liz volunteered. "That way if you need anything—"

"No, it's okay," he said, cutting her off. "I don't want you to waste the rest of the day baby-sitting me."

He meant it. She could see that. He wasn't just trying to be nice.

"Okay, well . . . I'll see you later, then." Liz stood up slowly so she wouldn't jar him. She thought about leaning over to kiss him good-bye, but it would probably just hurt him.

"Bye," Max said.

Liz felt a little shiver skitter through her when she realized that even though he was talking to her, he was already halfway back into the deep connection. Without another word, she turned around and rushed out of the house, glad to step into the sunshine.

As she headed to the bus stop, she broke into a run. She didn't plan to, but it just felt right. Suddenly she had to get away from Max's house as fast as possible. Her dark hair streamed behind her as she pushed herself faster and faster, pulling in breath after breath of the cool air.

When she reached the stop, the bus was just pulling up. The door wheezed open, and Liz occupied herself digging out the right change and depositing it. Then she took a seat and stared out the window. As the bus rolled down the street, she forced herself to look at each building, each little store in each little strip mall. She just wanted to blank out for a while. Not think. About anything.

When the bus got close to the Crashdown Café, her father's restaurant, she reached out and rang the buzzer. She'd been planning to hook up with Michael and Maria, but—

But the Crashdown stop is the same stop as the UFO museum, and you want to see Adam, a knowing little voice inside her head informed her.

I don't want to see Adam, Liz told herself. But when she climbed off the bus, her feet turned toward the museum.

Okay, well, it's not like I *want* to see him, she amended. But I need to tell him that Kyle Valenti is going all stalker, trying to find out what happened to his father.

Oh yeah, right, the little voice retorted. Why

does Adam need to know that? Kyle Valenti has no idea Adam even exists. And besides, Michael and Adam are roommates. Michael will tell Adam everything he needs to know.

"I'm not going to be one of those people who has these conversations with herself," Liz muttered, glad no one was on the sidewalk to hear her.

Fine, I'll be quiet, the little voice answered. As soon as you admit you want to see Adam. Can't wait to see him. Because when Adam looks at you, it's like you're the most beautiful, wonderful person he's ever seen.

It's just the way Max used to look at you.


"Honey, I'm home," Michael yelled as he unlocked the apartment door.

"Okay, honey, I'm in the kitchen," Adam called back. There wasn't a trace of sarcasm in his voice. That was what happened when you'd lived most of your life underground with only picture books from Dad Valenti to read and no TV or Internet access. You took everything way too friggin' literally.

"Uh, Adam, I was just joking around when I called you honey, okay?" he explained as he entered the kitchen and took a seat at the table. "Don't get the idea that that's the way guys usually, you know, address each other or anything."

"How long is it going to take me to get all this stuff?" Adam burst out. "I spend all day studying, trying to catch up and become seminormal, and I still—"

"The joking thing makes it confusing," Michael interrupted. "Besides, this is Roswell. You qualified as seminormal around here about your second day. On the way to Maria's brother's basketball game, Maria and I saw a guy wearing his underpants on the outside and a T-shirt that said Abductee Volunteer."

Adam gave a snort of laughter. "You want some cereal?" he asked, holding up his own bowl of little oat rockets and marshmallow planets.

"I'll pass," Michael answered. He tilted his chair back on two legs and opened the fridge. He studied the contents for a minute, then pulled out a plate of cold spaghetti and a squeeze bottle of chocolate sauce. When he'd slammed the fridge closed and turned back to the table, he saw Adam looking at him with a worried expression.

"What?" Michael mumbled through his first bite.

"Is it normal to eat cereal for dinner?" Adam asked.

"You're a guy living on your own. It's totally normal," Michael told him. "And anyway, being too normal isn't normal."

He was careful to keep his voice low and casual even though a flare of anger had gone off inside him. If Sheriff Valenti wasn't already dead, Michael would cheerfully kill him for what he'd done to Adam. The guy couldn't even eat a bowl of cereal without feeling like a freak.

"Can I ask you something else?" Adam sat down across from Michael. "I'm trying to figure out the kissing thing."

"The kissing thing," Michael repeated. "O-kay, go ahead."

"Friends kiss each other sometimes, right?" Adam said. He shoveled a couple of spoonfuls of cereal into his mouth.

"Right," Michael agreed. "Well, guy-girl friends or sometimes girl-girl friends. Not guy-guy friends," he added quickly. He decided not to go into the whole gay-straight issue since Adam was still trying to get down the basics.

"But it's a different kind of kissing, right?" Adam asked.

"Right," Michael said again. He didn't mind answering a few questions, but he hoped Adam wasn't expecting some kind of birds-and-bees sex talk. If he was, Michael would just tell him to start watching a little more cable.

"How's it different? That's what I need to know." Adam scooped up the last of the cereal, then drained the milk at the bottom of the bowl.

Michael thought it over for a minute. "Location, mainly. If you kiss a friend, it's usually not on the lips. And if it is on the lips, then it's a tongue issue. There is no tongue penetration." He picked up a hunk of cold spaghetti, and plopped it into his mouth. He followed it with a chocolate-sauce chaser.

"But lips with no tongue would be okay," Adam said. "Like you've kissed Maria that way."

"Yeah," Michael answered. He didn't add that he'd also kissed Maria that *other* way. And enjoyed it immensely. If he told Adam that, Adam would just get confused. He wouldn't get why Michael and Maria were just friends if they—

"Okay, say you kissed someone in the friends way, but then *they* used their tongue. Does that make it okay for you to use yours?" Adam asked. He gave his cereal bowl a spin and almost knocked it off the table.

"It depends," Michael answered. "If you only want to be friends with the girl, then you shouldn't because if you did, the girl would think you were up for being more than friends. It's a girl thing," he explained. "But if you want to be more than friends, then yeah, totally, go for it."

"So if you kissed Maria, and she—"

"Wait," Michael interrupted. "You're not interested in Maria, are you?" Michael knew he wasn't with Maria or anything, but the idea of Adam trying to start something up with her was unacceptable.

Adam shook his head. "It was just an example."

Michael did a quick aura check. He didn't see any signs of deception in the yellow glow around Adam.

"But you are interested in someone, aren't you?" Michael asked.

The rim of Adam's aura darkened to a deep orange, and his face flushed. "Not really," he muttered.

*You are such a humongous liar,* Michael thought. But he didn't call Adam on it.

It's not like it would be all that hard to figure who Adam had a thing for. He pretty much only knew three girls—Maria, Isabel, and Liz.

*Adam's cruising toward a broken heart,* Michael thought. *Isabel does love him, but she loves him in a protective way, like a little brother.*

*And Liz. Liz was with Max. Hearts and flowers. Now and forever. All that Harlequin romance bull.*

*Adam didn't stand a chance with Liz.*

Adam flopped down on the air mattress in the corner of the living room, and his thoughts, as always, turned to Liz.

He couldn't help it. And the fact that she'd stopped by the museum that afternoon only made it harder to stop. She'd only stayed for about three minutes. He hadn't even been able to convince her to sit down and relax. But in those three minutes he'd gone into sensory overload. The color of her lips, the smell of her hair when she walked past him, the sound of her voice. The combination had packed such a punch that he'd been practically on his knees by the time she left.

Even so, he wished she'd stayed longer. Tortured him some more.

Maybe then he could have figured out what was bothering her. He knew something was, and not just the fact that Kyle Valenti had threatened the group.

*Something was bothering her the other night when I went into her dream, too,* he remembered. She'd been in the middle of a horrible nightmare.

Adam rolled over onto his side and peered at his watch. It was after one. Liz was probably already asleep. Was she having bad dreams again? Because if she was, it would be a friend kind of thing to go into her dream and stop it, right?

*I'll just check on her,* Adam decided. *If she's okay, I'll leave.*

He closed his eyes and allowed all the muscles in his body to relax and soften. A moment later the dream orbs appeared, whirling, translucent spheres of every color imaginable. They were all beautiful, but there was only one that held any attraction for Adam.

He whistled, long and low, and Liz's dream orb came to him. It circled around his head until he reached up and gently caught it between his hands. He pulled apart his palms, and the orb expanded to the size of a beach ball.

*Just a quick look,* Adam promised himself again, unable to completely get rid of the sweaty-guilty feeling that he was doing something wrong. He peered into the orb and saw Liz sitting at her desk. It looked like she was filling out college applications.

Not exactly a wonderful dream, but not a nightmare, either. Adam locked his eyes on Liz, wanting to soak up as many details as he could. The shape of the little hollow at the base of her throat. The way she'd tucked her hair behind her ear on one side and let it fall free on the other. The way the polish on her fingernails was a shade lighter than the polish on her toenails.

Wait. When he looked at her feet, he thought he saw something. Adam jerked apart his hands, forcing the walls of the orb out. His heart thudded hard against his chest. A couple of inches of water covered the floor, and the water level was rising. Fast.

Almost as soon as Adam realized this, the water was up to Liz's knees. She jumped up from the chair and started wading toward the door. Before she got halfway there, the water was to her waist, then her chest. Liz forced herself forward, using her arms to help propel herself through the water. She grabbed the door handle and pulled. But the pressure of the water was too strong. She couldn't get the door open.

Enough! Adam thought. He did the first thing he could think of. He used his mind to reconfigure Liz's body, turning her into a goldfish.

Liz immediately started darting around, exploring, enjoying her fish self. Adam let out a breath he didn't even know he was holding. She was okay.

Adam knew he should go now. He'd done what he needed to do. But he couldn't resist turning her bed into one of those ceramic castles he'd seen in fishbowls at the pet store.

He smiled as she shimmied through one of the windows and then swam out the front door. She's all set, he thought. Just go.

But how much fun could a castle be for one fish all by herself? Adam said to himself. She needed a friend. There was nothing wrong with hanging out with Liz as friends, especially if they were both fish.

He stretched out his arms as far as they would go, expanding Liz's dream orb until it was large enough for him to step through. As soon as he was inside, he transformed himself into a goldfish, too.

Liz swam around one of the castle's turrets, spotted him, and then dove straight toward him.

When she reached him, she gave him a playful poke in the side with her goldfish snout. Then she flicked herself around and darted into the castle. A second later he spotted her looking out one of the windows. Looking for him.

Adam didn't need an engraved invitation. So what if they were both fish? So what if Liz had no idea who he was? They were together, and that was all he cared about.

# THREE

Michael finished the last problem for his calc class and shut the book. Now what? He still had a few hours before he'd be ready to go to sleep.

He wandered into the living room. Adam was stretched out in the corner. He had the zonked-out, vacant expression that let Michael know he was off in the dream plane. Michael wondered whose orb he was in.

I should give him some suggestions later, Michael thought. He didn't know the orbs of practically everyone in town the way Isabel did, but he'd still managed to discover some that usually had some interesting stuff going on.

Michael headed down the spiral staircase that led to the museum and looked around. Pretty soon the place would be ready for a grand reopening. Smiling, Michael walked over to the information counter and grabbed a piece of paper and a pencil. When the museum opened its doors again, he was going to be the boss. He was going to be *Max's* boss. Cool.

Leaning against the counter, Michael started a list. (1) Call old employees. (2) Go over account books. (3) Order supplies for coffee shop. Is there enough cash for a cappuccino machine? (4) Come up with killer display for front window.

He wanted something that would make everyone in town come in, even if they'd been to the museum a million times already. But what? He let out a snort. He'd be the best-possible display. He'd have lines out the wazoo if he put a real, live alien in the window. But obviously there were a few little problems with that idea. Like potential imprisonment. Like potential death.

Measurements. Before he could make any decisions, he needed measurements so he'd know exactly how much space he had to work with. He leaned across the counter and opened the long drawer in the middle, then rooted around until he found a tape measure.

Maybe I can set up some kind of multimedia deal, he thought as he made his way over to the window and stepped up into the narrow display area. A video loop. Maybe I could—

All his thoughts disappeared as he felt a prickling sensation at the back of his neck. The little hairs were standing on end, just the way they had at the game when Kyle Valenti was staring at him and Maria.

Slowly he turned his head and peered out at the dark, empty street. He actually saw a little better at night than he did in the day, so he instantly spotted the guy pressed up against the snow cone shack in the parking lot almost directly across from the museum.

The guy had his face angled away from Michael, but Michael recognized the build and the longish brown hair. It was Kyle Valenti.

Big mistake, rat boy, he thought. This is the perfect time and place for me to deal with you. Michael stepped out of the display window, trying to make it look natural.

As soon as he was out of Kyle's sight line, he sprinted to the back door and slipped outside. He circled behind the museum and the jewelry store next door, then inched up to the sidewalk and shot a look across the street. Kyle was still there.

"Ready or not, here I come," Michael whispered. He launched himself at Kyle, running full out. He lowered his shoulder and rammed Kyle to the ground before rat boy even had a chance to turn around.

Michael grabbed both of Kyle's wrists and pinned them behind his back.

"You just keep eating pavement until we're finished with our little chat. You got that, Kyle?" Michael demanded. He jabbed his knee into the loser's back just to make his point clear.

"I'm not Kyle," the guy said, his words muffled against the asphalt of the parking lot.

"What?" Michael grabbed the guy by the shoulders and flipped him over.

He wasn't lying. He definitely wasn't Kyle. This

guy looked more like Michael than he did like Kyle. Michael shoved himself to his feet, then leaned down and helped the guy up.

"Sorry," he said. "Someone's been following me, and I thought you were him. Are you okay?"

"Yeah," the guy answered, his gray eyes never leaving Michael's face.

What does he want from me? I said I was sorry, Michael thought.

"So, uh, are you waiting for the bus or something?" he asked. "The stop's a couple of blocks that way." He jerked his chin to the right.

"You're Michael Guerin, aren't you?" the guy asked.

The prickling started up at the back of Michael's neck again, but this time it kept moving until it got all the way to his knees.

"That's right," Michael answered.

For another long moment the stranger just looked at him in silence, causing Michael's adrenaline to start pumping all over again. What did this guy *want*?

"I'm your brother," he finally said.

Michael's heart responded with a nervous thud, but he ignored it. The guy was obviously wacko.

"Brother," Michael repeated. Just forming the word felt awkward. It was as if his lips and tongue had been shot full of novocaine. "Bull," he exploded. "I don't have a brother."

Ray Iburg had told Michael that he didn't have any family on the home planet. No brothers, no sisters, no nothing.

The guy didn't answer, but a moment later Michael felt the sizzle of power in the air. He had to concentrate to keep his knees from buckling. Whoever this guy was, he had power.

That meant he was one of them.

The sizzling, electric sensation intensified. Michael started building a power ball of his own. He had to be ready for a counterattack.

"You want to play, we can play," Michael muttered.

A cracking sound filled the empty street. Michael jerked his head toward the noise and saw the three-foot-high alien on top of the snow cone shack pull free of the shack's roof. It shot straight up into the air, and it didn't come back down. It just kept on flying. Michael kept his eyes on it until it was out of sight.

"Impressive," he commented, making sure to keep his voice low and even. He continued to build up his power ball. He wasn't letting his guard down until he knew what the deal was here.

"You still don't believe me, do you?" the guy demanded. Before Michael could answer, the guy shot out his hand and grabbed Michael by the wrist.

The connection was instantaneous. But instead of the blast of images Michael usually got when he connected with someone, he found himself on the home planet. At least it matched up with the species memories of home that had always been a part of him.

He knew he wasn't actually there, but every sensation seemed completely authentic. The wisps of acidic mist coming off the lake sent tingles through his skin. The scent of the fruit from the nearby trees was thick and rich in his nose, making his mouth water. He could feel the slow beats of his primary heart and the faster, double thumps of his secondary appendage.

Wait. What? Secondary appendage. Michael didn't even know what that was.

No, that wasn't true. It was like he had two brains now. His Michael brain. And this other brain, a brain that knew exactly what a secondary appendage was, a brain that knew exactly where on the planet he was, a brain that even remembered diving into that lake over there with his father.

His father. Michael felt dizzy. He had no memories of his father. His father had died before Michael broke free of his pod.

What was going on?

He ran his hands down his body, realizing several things at once. His arms were much shorter, his fingers now tapered into hooked claws, and his skin was hard and bumpy. He glanced down at himself and saw what looked like rows and rows of metal rivets where his flesh should be.

What the *hell* was going on?

He heard the patter of light footsteps behind him, and he spun around. Two beings with small bodies, big heads, and dark, dark, pupil-less almond-shaped eyes approached him. The Michael part of his brain thought it recognized them from the hologram of the ship's crew Ray Iburg had once shown him. The non-Michael part of his brain recognized them, too—as its parents.

"We have to leave you now, my son," one of the beings said. The words weren't spoken in English, but the non-Michael part of the brain supplied the translation and identified the speaker—Father.

Michael felt a rush of grief that was from him but not from him. He told himself not to freak and to try to absorb everything being said.

"If it were known your father and I had produced another pod, it would be destroyed," the other being—Mother—told him. "We must find a safe place for your brother to be born, a place where our family will be able to live together without hiding."

"Why can't I come with you?" Michael asked, although he hadn't intended to speak the words, wouldn't have known how to speak them if he had wanted to.

"No one on the ship must know that the pod we bring with us is not our first. No one must know that we already have a child," Father explained.

"But I promise that we will return for you as soon as we are able. And I promise that you will be safe with the members of the Kindred until then."

Father reached out and squeezed his shoulder. Mother ran two of her long fingers down his face. Then they were gone.

And Michael was back in his own body, back in front of the snow cone stand across the street from the museum. He scrubbed his face with his hands, trying to get rid of the woozy, disoriented feeling swamping him.

The dark-haired guy was simply watching Michael, waiting.

Michael pressed his fingers against his forehead for a moment. He could almost feel his brain trying to process what he'd experienced.

"I—I was in you just then, you when you were a little kid, right?" Michael stammered.

"Yes," the guy answered, his gray eyes steady as they met Michael's.

"So, then . . ." Michael stopped, took a breath. Then he forced himself to spit out the words, the words he'd never imagined he would say to anyone. "So then you really are my brother."

Isabel was so bored, she could scream.

She still had a couple of hours to go before it was time for her two hours of sleep. She'd already reorganized the kitchen cabinets and done her nails—three times so she could decide which was exactly the right Isabel-esque shade of polish. She'd even used her power to soften the skin on her elbows and her knees, not that they needed it.

I could write another letter to Alex, she thought.

Another letter explaining how sorry she was about the nasty way she'd broken up with him. Another letter explaining how much she loved him, even though they weren't boyfriend and girlfriend anymore.

Another letter that he'd never get.

Isabel wrapped her arms around herself. She didn't want to think about Alex. Not now. Not in the middle of the night when she was all alone. She knew she'd only end up crying. And once she started, she wasn't sure she'd ever be able to stop.

Usually on a night like this, she would insist that Max come downstairs and amuse her. But when she'd gone into Max's room an hour ago, he was bye-bye, off with the consciousness.

It was like her brother had joined a cult or something. And he couldn't wait for her to join, too. Maybe I should call one of those psychics and ask for advice, Isabel thought.

Or maybe she should just go upstairs and shake Max out of his trance. Yeah, he'd been talking to his little friends long enough. Isabel stood up and strolled down the hall and over to the stairs. She had her foot on the first step when she heard a soft knock on the door.

Yes! Michael or Adam had come to save her from terminal ennui. It had to be one of them—no one else would show up at this time of night.

She spun around, rushed back down the hall to the front door, and flung it open.

"Do you think you could have gotten here a little sooner?" she demanded.

And then she realized it wasn't Michael standing there. It wasn't Adam, either.

It was Alex.

Oh, God, it was Alex.

"Are you? What? I—" Isabel's brain was too scrambled to complete a thought. She squeezed her eyes shut for a second, trying to get a grip, then she opened them and a smile spread across her face, a smile so big, it felt like it was stretching all the way to the back of her head. "Just get in here," she said.

Alex took a step forward, then he did a slow crumple to the porch.

Isabel dropped to her knees beside him. She shoved her hands under his shirt and pressed them against his chest. Her heart gave a painful jerk as she realized how cold and moist his skin felt.

Just make the connection, she ordered herself. She stared down into Alex's green eyes, and she was in. But she couldn't focus on the images from Alex's life flying past her. She was freezing, her entire body so chilled, it almost burned—as if it had been rubbed with dry ice.

42

No, not her body. *Their* body. She and Alex had only one body now.

Why is he so cold? she thought. What's wrong? She explored their body slowly and methodically, ignoring the spikes of ice digging into her.

There were no foreign substances in the bloodstream. Alex didn't have a virus or anything that was giving him chills. Isabel directed her attention to his—their—brain, tracing the neural pathways.

Suddenly the images from Alex stopped coming. All she could see was blackness. Then a single image formed. Alex screaming, an endless scream, his face twisted in fear.

He's terrified, she realized. There was no external cause for the condition of his body. He'd been frightened so deeply that his internal systems had started to shut down.

What happened to him? What did he see? What did the beings do to him?

Not the time for questions, Isabel ordered herself. Alex needed her healing. But there wasn't a specific place to direct her powers.

Isabel drew as much strength and energy from herself as she could, then she let it fly into Alex. Was it enough? She pulled her hands away, breaking the connection.

She would have loved to stay connected, to stay that close to Alex. But she had to get Max.

43

"Can you stand up?" she asked. She brushed his hair off his forehead.

"Yeah." Alex shoved himself to his feet, and Isabel looped her arm around his waist and half carried him over to the sofa. It's Alex, her brain gibbered. It's Alex, Alex, Alex, it's my Alex.

"Just lie here for a minute." She grabbed the Indian blanket off the back of the chair and wrapped it tightly around him. "Don't move. I'll be right back," she whispered.

This was definitely not a situation that she wanted the parents involved in. Fortunately they were both pretty heavy sleepers.

"Miss you," Alex mumbled. Isabel didn't know if he meant that he'd miss her when she went up-stairs or that he'd missed her when he was gone.

"Miss you, too," she answered, meaning it both ways.

She turned around, ran up to Max's room, and dashed inside without bothering to knock. One look at his face showed her that he was still con-nected. Isabel grabbed the pillow off his bed and whacked him across the head.

"Max," she hissed. "I need you. Right now!"

Max's eyelids fluttered open, then he lifted his head and stared at her.

"Did you just hit me with a pillow?" he asked, sounding confused.

"Alex is back," Isabel exclaimed. "He's down-stairs."

Max leaped to his feet and was out the door before Isabel could say another word. She followed him as he raced to the living room. He stopped so abruptly when he reached the sofa that Isabel slammed into his back.

"I can't believe it's really you," Max said softly. Alex gave a weak smile.

"Me either," Isabel answered. She reached out and stroked Alex's face. His skin felt a little warmer, but he was still way too pale.

"Should I start debating whether Lime Warp or Blast! is truly the most superior alien-themed beverage?" Alex joked, his voice coming out thin and hoarse.

"It's him." Max dropped into the chair next to the sofa and leaned toward Alex. "So what happened? How'd you make it back?"

"You have to tell us everything," Isabel agreed. She stepped over the coffee table and sat down as close to Alex as she could get.

"I will," Alex promised. He struggled to a sitting position, then leaned his head on the back of the sofa, as if the effort had exhausted him. "As much as I can remember, anyway, which isn't a lot. But first you've got to know that we may be getting company."

"Go on," Max said, his eyes serious and watchful. He'd clearly heard the urgency in Alex's voice, just as Isabel had.

Alex lifted his head. His eyes looked clearer to Isabel now. More focused.

"I don't know how exactly, but I was in a wormhole," he began. "I could see . . . space, outer space, all around me in a blur, but I could breathe and everything, and I—" He stopped himself, his expression turning hard and grim. "That's not the important part. When I was in the hole, something came after me. I think . . . I think it might have followed me here."

That's what terrified him—whatever was in the hole, Isabel thought. She reached out and took Alex's right hand in both of hers, then started rubbing.

"Here earth or here this house?" Isabel asked, struggling to keep her voice low.

"I'm not sure," Alex admitted. "I came here because I didn't know if I could handle it alone. I thought maybe there'd be need of some—some firepower, and I didn't want to lead *whatever* to my parents. Sorry."

Isabel traded Alex's left hand for his right and kept rubbing.

"Don't be sorry," Max told him. "You did the right thing. If something does go down, Isabel and I can combine powers."

"Do you have any clue what it was?" Isabel asked. She shot a glance toward the front door, even though she was too far away to see anything out of the long, narrow window that ran alongside it.

"I didn't see it—I just *felt* it," Alex answered. "And I'm pretty sure it wanted something from me. I think it would have killed me to get it."

"Do you still feel it?" Max asked, his eyes intent on Alex.

Alex hesitated. "I don't feel it coming after me," he said slowly. "But I don't think it's gone." He shook his head. "Maybe it didn't exist at all. Maybe my imagination is just out of control."

"I don't think so," Max answered.

Isabel gave him a sharp look. "You know something about this?" she demanded.

Max stood up and began to pace back and forth in front of the coffee table.

"I'm not sure," he said. "The consciousness has been in total upheaval tonight. It's been like a bunch of tidal waves crashing through. I was trying to get some idea of what was happening, but all the beings were too devastated to give me any info." He stopped in front of Alex. "There could be a connection."

"The beings wanted me to go back," Alex said. "They sent me."

"Maybe something went wrong when they opened the hole. I'll try to deepen the connection later, see what I can find out." Max started to pace again. "You're staying here tonight," he told Alex in his big-brother-has-spoken tone. "I'll go get you a sleeping bag out of the garage." He strode out of the room.

47

Isabel pressed herself tighter against Alex's side. It didn't feel close enough, even though she was so close, she could feel the tiny tremors rippling through him.

He was still seriously freaked. She twisted her body around until she was half facing him, then wrapped her arms around his waist and held on tight.

"You're home," she whispered, burying her head in his shoulder, breathing in the scent of him. "Nothing can hurt you now that you're home."

# FUR

"How long have I been gone?" Alex asked as Max pulled out of the driveway and onto the street the next morning.

"Maybe two weeks," Isabel told him.

Two weeks. Only two weeks. He could hardly twist his mind around that.

"I hope someone taped *Oprah* for me, or I'm going to be seriously pissed," Alex joked. "I'm not going to be able to keep up my rep as a sensitive guy if I don't know what Oprah's doing." Isabel and Max laughed. Alex laughed, too, even though he usually thought it was lame to laugh at your own jokes. He couldn't help it. It just felt too good to be riding down the streets of his dinky little town with two of his best friends. He was home.

"I hope everyone's already at Michael's," Isabel said as Max turned down the road toward the museum. "They can't wait to see you."

"Yeah, and Michael said something about having a big announcement to make," Max added, glancing at Alex in the rearview mirror. "Although I don't know what could be bigger than having you back."

"Yeah, I am pretty huge," Alex joked, stretching out his arms.

Isabel shook her head but giggled. "Looks like Maria's here, at least," she commented as Max pulled into the museum parking lot.

"Get ready for some major squealing," Max told Alex. He pulled to a stop by the stairs leading up to Michael and Adam's apartment.

Almost on cue, the door to the apartment flew open. "Alex!" Maria screeched. She took the stairs three at a time, Liz right behind her.

Alex scrambled out of the Jeep and started to run as soon as his feet touched the pavement. His legs were still a little weak, but running was the only option. He was about a third of the way up the stairs when Liz and Maria reached him. He didn't know whose arms were wrapped around him or who was kissing him, and he didn't care.

"Come on! Come upstairs," Liz exclaimed. She and Maria each took one of his hands, and they all squeezed up the staircase without losing their grips on each other.

"Okay, break it up, break it up," Michael called as they pushed through the front door. He waved them into the living room. When Alex passed by, Michael gave him a fast, hard hug.

"Good to have you back," he said, not quite looking Alex in the eye.

"Thanks," Alex answered. He felt a tentative

hand on his shoulder, and then suddenly Adam had him in a half hug, half choke hold.

"We've been trying to get you home," Adam said as he released Alex.

"Yeah, we almost did," Liz added.

"It was so close. We tracked DuPris to the caverns—I figured that part out," Maria jumped in.

"Excuse me. I think I had something to do with it," Isabel said from behind him.

Alex gazed from person to person, soaking up the sight of them. Liz, Maria, Michael, and—some strange guy.

"Clearly I missed something more than a few *Oprah* eps," he said. "I'm Alex, but I guess you figured that out," he told the guy.

"I'm Trevor, or at least that's close enough to my name," the guy answered after a glance at Michael. He reached out and shook Alex's hand.

Alex got a fuzzy, unpleasant twinge of déjà vu. He tried to figure out if he'd ever seen the guy before. There was something familiar about him.

"I'm guessing Trevor is part of this announcement," Max said to Michael.

So the others don't know him, either, Alex realized.

"He's pretty much the whole thing," Michael answered. "I know this is going to sound bizarre. I mean, I know I'm not even supposed to have one. At least that's what—wait, maybe I should start with—see, I could feel what Trevor—" He started laughing, laughing so hard, he started to choke and snort. "I sound like Maria."

This is a change, Alex thought. Michael was acting, well, *silly* was the only word for it. Alex had seen Michael be sarcastic lots of times. And Michael definitely wasn't a guy to step away from gross-out humor. But silly—that just wasn't him.

"And what's wrong with acting like me?" Maria asked, hands on her hips in mock indignation. Michael laughed harder.

Alex smiled. He felt himself entering the sappy zone again. Maria being Maria was a pretty enjoyable sight. So was Michael being not Michael.

"If you don't stop giggling like you're deranged or something and tell us whatever you dragged us here to tell us right now—," Isabel threatened.

"All right. All right." Michael pulled in a deep breath. "I'll just say it—Trevor is my brother."

"How can that be possible?" Liz asked.

"Your brother?" Isabel exclaimed at the same time. "Your *brother*?"

"Wait, there are even more of you?" Maria blurted out, her words overlapping with Liz and Isabel's. "Not that that's a bad thing," she added quickly.

"Start at the beginning," Max instructed, his eyes darting between Michael and Trevor. "Tell us everything."

Alex didn't say anything. He was still trying to

figure out why Trevor seemed so familiar. Just standing near him was making Alex uneasy, sort of tense and restless.

Michael started explaining, and he was talking so fast, Alex could hardly understand him. Alex wished he had the ability to see auras. He bet at that moment Michael's was awesome, bursting with the colors of absolute joy.

Alex wouldn't mind seeing Trevor's aura right then, too. Maybe if he could see Trevor's aura, it would reassure Alex that the guy was . . . okay.

"Anyway, they left Trevor with this group called the Kindred," Michael was saying. "Or at least what translates to the Kindred in English. It's a group that believes that people should be able to have as many children as they want."

"They just left you there?" Maria asked Trevor. Her blue eyes were warm with sympathy.

Alex used the interruption to head over to a stack of flattened beanbag chairs along the nearest wall. He sat down, positioning himself so that he still had a clear view of Trevor. The muscles in his stomach relaxed a little now that there was more distance between the two of them.

"Our parents were going to go back and get me once they found a safe place, a place where they wouldn't have to keep one of their kids in hiding," Trevor explained. His eyes were on Alex, even though he was answering Maria's question.

Alex met his gaze as long as possible, but finally he had to look away when he felt hot bile begin to rise up his throat.

Michael reached out and squeezed Trevor's shoulder. "You all know the rest of the story," Michael said.

Michael and Trevor's parents had died in the crash, the crash that had made Roswell the T-shirt-selling, green-food-producing tourist attraction it was today. Sometimes Alex wondered what it would be like to live in a town that made most of its money off your parents' death, practically celebrated it, even.

"So, how did you get here?" Max finally asked after they'd all taken a moment to absorb what Michael had said. Max walked over and sat down next to Alex. The burst of relief that spread through Alex made him feel like a total wimp. What—he didn't feel safe without Max around to protect him?

"I knew that my parents had died on earth and that my brother had survived and was living in Roswell under the name Michael Guerin. Members of the Kindred were able to get me that information," Trevor explained.

"You just got here yesterday?" Liz asked. She plopped down across from Max and Alex and gestured for the others to join them.

"Just off the boat," Trevor joked. He positioned himself on Alex's other side. It took all Alex's self-control not to flinch.

"How do you know English and everything?"

Adam asked, plopping down next to Isabel.

"The Kindred also got me the materials I needed to teach myself English and the local behavioral norms," Trevor explained. "I always dreamed about coming here, but I never thought I'd be able to until—"

"Until the collective consciousness opened another wormhole to send Alex back," Michael jumped in. "Trevor basically hitched a ride here."

"Yeah, thanks," Trevor told Alex, giving him another long look.

Alex's stomach cramped until it felt about the size of a postage stamp. It was Trevor behind him in the wormhole. It was Trevor who had wanted something from Alex, something he would have killed Alex to get.

"That's one thing we don't have to worry about, then," Isabel said. "Alex felt something following him home, and we were afraid it might be dangerous."

Everyone laughed. Alex forced himself to laugh, too. But he knew what he felt from the being who followed him, from Trevor. A cold-blooded willingness to murder whatever stood in its—in his—way.

"I wish I could have been there to see you two meet. It must have been like a total soap opera moment," Max said. His tone was casual, but his blue eyes were cool and serious. He turned to Michael. "I'm surprised Trevor even managed to convince you of who he really was."

Max isn't sure Trevor is who he's pretending to be, either, Alex thought hopefully.

"What I don't get is how the consciousness managed to open the hole," Max continued. "I asked if they could open one to get Alex home, and what I got back was that they weren't strong enough and wouldn't be for a long time."

Trevor shrugged. "I just took advantage of it. I don't know how they did it. I'm not connected to the consciousness." He shot a probing glance at Alex.

Alex forced himself to look straight back. But he was the first one to glance away again.

"No idea," Alex said. "I think that my memory got wiped. I remember being sucked up the wormhole instead of DuPris. And I remember flying back through it. But not much in between—just kind of shapes and muffled sounds."

Alex hoped no one could tell he was lying. He did have a pretty good idea how the consciousness had gotten the strength to send him home.

Trying to look casual, he slipped his hand into his pocket and wrapped his fingers around the Stone of Midnight.

When he'd arrived back home, he'd had the Stone—one of the three—with him. He was sure it was the power of the Stone that had opened the hole.

He had intended to give the stone to Max, but he'd passed out last night before he'd had the chance. There was no way he was going to hand it over right now. Not until he was a lot more sure what, exactly, Trevor's deal was.

"Uh, now that I know the boogeyman in the hole with me was only Michael's brother, I guess it's safe to go home and tell my parents I'm still alive," Alex said.

"I'll drive you," Max volunteered.

"I'll go, too," Liz offered. She smiled at Trevor. "I want to hear everything about you later."

Me too, Alex silently added. But first he was going to put the Stone somewhere safe until he could figure out what to do next.

"Alex, there's something you need to know before you go home," Liz said as soon as they were on the road. She turned around so she could look at him, and the worried expression on her face had his stomach going from postage stamp to pea.

"Your dad . . . ." Liz hesitated, and Alex's brain went nuts. His dad what? Had disowned him? Had had a heart attack? Had finally shouted one too many times and spontaneously combusted?

"Tell me," he demanded.

"Your dad is with Project Clean Slate," she blurted out.

Alex felt like he was crashing through another wormhole.

"We found out because he was trying to get you back, too," Max explained, shooting a fast glance over his shoulder.

"Wait. My dad was looking for me?" Alex asked. He found that sort of hard to believe. Maybe the garage needed cleaning or something.

"Yeah," Max answered. "Your dad had tracked down DuPris to try to suck up some power from the Stone with a Clean Slate device, and we'd tracked down DuPris to try to steal the Stone. We sort of ran into each other."

"But he didn't find out the truth, obviously," Alex said. He leaned forward, bracing his hands on the roll bar, and turned to Max. "I mean you, Isabel, Michael, and Adam are all still walking around free."

He couldn't imagine anything worse than his own father holding his friends captive, the way Sheriff Valenti had imprisoned Adam.

"Actually, he does know," Liz replied. "It was pretty much unavoidable. But he helped us escape from DuPris."

"Yeah, you missed out on DuPris's latest attempt to kill us all," Max said as he swung the Jeep onto Alex's street.

"And your dad said we were wrong about what Clean Slate's agenda was," Liz explained.

The shreds of Alex's brain that remained were screaming from information overload. "So, then, what is its agenda?"

Max pulled into Alex's driveway and parked. "We don't know," he admitted.

Great, Alex thought. One more thing to worry about. What a homecoming.

"Doesn't Doug Highsinger realize that he has a better chance of getting his precious Mustang dinged when he takes up two parking places?" Max muttered as he maneuvered the Jeep into a tight space in the school parking lot.

Liz muffled a sigh. Max wasn't in one of his deep connections with the consciousness, but he wasn't exactly focused on her, either. It's not that she expected him to worship her and never think of anything except her. She didn't expect him to be Adam or anything, but—

Whoa. Where did that thought come from?

It comes from the fact that when you're in a room with Adam, you're his whole world, answered the obnoxious little voice that seemed to have taken up residence inside Liz's head.

Liz ignored it. She reached into her backpack, pulled out a brown paper sack, and thrust it into Max's hands.

He opened the top and gave a long sniff. "Blueberry and jalapeño. "You made them just for me?" Max said, sounding like it was this big deal.

Liz got an unexpected burst of what-an-excellent-girlfriend-I-am pleasure. It was only marred by the fact that she knew she'd made the muffins as soon as she got home from visiting

Adam yesterday, in a session of somewhat guilt-induced baking. "You're pretty much the only one who'd eat them," she reminded him.

Max wrapped her ponytail around his fist and gently urged her head back. Then he leaned over and kissed her, kissed her in a way that made her feel like she was his whole universe.

Now that Alex is back, everything's going to be different, Liz thought when Max lifted his lips from hers. Max wouldn't have to connect in that deep way anymore.

"I always thought that saying 'the way to a man's heart is through his stomach' was sexist propaganda," she said, still a little breathless from that amazing kiss. "But I guess not."

"I do love the taste of those muffins," he teased. He paused, then added, "But I love the taste of you more."

Liz grabbed Max's T-shirt and pulled him back toward her, and they were kissing again. It felt so good. So right. As if some missing piece of herself had miraculously been found.

Liz slipped one hand around to the sweet spot at the back of Max's neck. He gave her bottom lip a playful nibble.

Then his lips went slack.

Liz pulled away slowly. When she looked into Max's eyes, they were blank. Her stomach dropped down to her toes, a wave of revulsion sweeping through her.

He'd gone into a deep connection right in the middle of kissing her. Had the beings been able to *feel* the kiss? Feel the sensation of her lips and tongue?

Liz yanked the neck of her T-shirt up until it covered her mouth, then she scrubbed, and scrubbed, and scrubbed. When she finished, the top of the T-shirt was stained with plum lipstick, and her lips felt raw.

She shot a glance at Max. At the Max *thing*. Because it definitely wasn't Max over there, not entirely, at least. It wasn't the guy who'd just made her feel like they were the only two people alive, living in their own Garden of Eden.

Liz reached for the door handle, then hesitated. "I can't just leave him here like this," she muttered. "There might be something really wrong."

She'd never seen Max have quite that reaction to connecting before, not that sudden clicking off. She forced herself to watch him until she could see his awareness of his surroundings, of her, return.

That little episode had nothing to do with Alex, Liz told herself. She had to accept that Max had changed after he went through his *akino*. His connection to the consciousness was the most powerful, intense thing in his life now.

"Sorry," he said. "I just got this massive flood of . . . of emotion, basically, from the consciousness. I couldn't control it at all. It just took me over."

"Are you okay?" Liz made herself ask.

Just say yes so I can get out of here, she thought, shocking herself with the strength of her desire to get away from Max.

"Yeah," he answered, his voice a little thick, as if he'd been asleep. "I wish I knew what was going on. I think maybe it has something to do with one of the Stones of Midnight. But that's all I got. None of the beings have really taken the time to explain things to me." He angled his head so he could see her watch. "Was I out long?"

"Less than a minute," Liz said. She smoothed a stray section of hair back into her ponytail and reached for the door handle again.

"So we still have a little time to . . ." Max smiled as he slid one arm around her shoulders.

Another wave of revulsion rose up inside her, and Liz gave an involuntary shudder. "Actually, I have to go to the library before class." She climbed out of the Jeep, gave Max a quick wave, and bolted.

It wasn't that she didn't want to kiss Max again. Kissing Max was what she wanted more than anything.

But it hadn't been Max sitting next to her. Not really.

Alex heard a key turn in the lock. A moment later he heard the sound of his parents' voices, and something inside him twisted.

He stood up from the kitchen table. Before he

could reach the kitchen door, his parents walked in, each carrying a couple of bags of groceries.

His mother looked up, and both bags slipped out of her hands. "Alex?" His name came out in a long quaver.

"It's me, Mom," he answered, his own voice not completely steady.

"Alex?" she repeated. She stumbled toward him, her heel catching on a box of cookies that had fallen out of one of the bags. Alex reached out and grabbed her by the elbows to steady her, and her hands locked on his arms as if she never planned to let him go.

"I'm okay. Don't worry. I'm fine," he told her.

"Where were you?" she cried. Her fingers dug so deeply into his skin that Alex was sure they'd leave bruises. But he didn't try to pull away.

"I . . . I took a hike into the desert, and, I don't know, I think I got lost," Alex said, his explanation sounding even more lame than it had when he'd made it up. "I came to this cave. I don't even re-member going in there."

"Heatstroke," his father said in his most authori-tative I-am-the-Major tone.

"Yeah, maybe," Alex agreed, glancing at his father. "I don't think I brought enough water. Stupid, I know. And . . . and it took me a while to find my way back."

"Do you want something to eat?" his mom asked. "Or do you want to take a nap? You must be exhausted."

To Alex's horror, tears were spilling down his mother's face. In the Manes family, you were supposed to pretty much pretend that nothing got to you. The Major was the champion of that, and he expected them all to follow his example.

His father set his bags on the table, then took Alex's mom by the shoulders and gently pulled her away from Alex.

"Why don't you go freshen up?" he said. "I'll make scrambled eggs for all of us."

"I . . . all right." His mother snagged a paper towel off the roll over the sink and swabbed at her eyes as she hurried out of the room.

"Grab that stuff off the floor and stick some bread in the toaster, would you?" the Major asked.

Good to see you, too, Alex thought as he crouched down and picked up the bags of groceries and the cookies. He dropped everything on the table, then started rooting around in the closest bag for bread.

What the hell am I doing?

Alex let his hands fall to his sides. "I know that you know where I really was," he told his father. "I know you're Clean Slate."

The Major nodded. He stepped around Alex and pulled a carton of eggs out of the fridge, then he strode to the stove and pulled a frying pan out of the cabinet underneath it.

"I assume your memory was cleaned before you

were sent back," he said. He cracked an egg into the pan, then another.

"You assume correctly," Alex muttered. His father didn't tell him to speak up the way he usually did.

"I want you to get yourself checked out by a doctor. Just a precaution." His father cracked two more eggs, studied the pan, and then added three more. "Get me a fork."

Alex handed him a wooden spoon. "You don't want to burn your fingers."

"Thanks." The Major began to stir the eggs vigorously. "I've been thinking about the ROTC."

I haven't been home even half an hour, and he's already ragging on me, Alex thought. He doesn't care what happened to me. All he cares about is getting the bragging rights to having four sons in the military.

"You're old enough to take care of yourself," his father continued. He reached for the pepper with his free hand, still stirring with the other. "If you don't want to go into the program, it's your call."

Alex held very still. He wasn't sure, but he thought the Major had just told Alex that he missed him or that he was proud of him. Or maybe even that he loved him.

"That means a lot to me," Alex finally answered. It seemed like the right coded response to his father's coded message.

Alex turned around and pulled the bread out of

one of the grocery bags. He took out six pieces and stuck four in the toaster.

"Dad, before Mom comes back, I need you to tell me what the story is with Clean Slate," Alex said, staring down at the coils in the toaster as they turned from black to orange. "I mean, will you be going after my friends now?"

"Project Clean Slate is classified to the highest level," the Major answered. "But I will tell you that your friends have nothing to fear from us."

"And that's all you can say—even to me?" Alex challenged.

"Yes," his father said evenly. "Hand me some plates."

Alex pulled three plates out of the cabinet and passed them over. The toast popped up, and he added slices next to the eggs his father was dishing out. A moment later he heard his mother's heels clicking toward them. He didn't have much more time alone with his dad.

"I just want to say thanks for trying to get me back," he blurted out.

The Major turned to Alex and waited until Alex met his gaze. "I would do anything to keep you safe," his father answered, his voice coming out choked and harsh. "Anything. Don't you know that?"

I do now, Alex thought.

# FIVE

"I'm thinking I should go through a wormhole and back," Maria told Liz as they drove to the Crashdown Café for their afternoon shift.

"Why?" Liz asked. She reached over and pulled the wheel a little to the right. Maria had the tendency to let the car drift into the wrong lane when she got caught up in what she was saying.

"Because did you see how great Alex looked?" Maria asked. "Shampoo-commercial hair, soap-commercial skin. He even seemed a little more muscle-y or something. And Michael's brother? He could be on a billboard. I wouldn't mind seeing him a hundred feet tall."

Liz made another small adjustment to the wheel. "If we ever figure out how to open a wormhole ourselves, we can start a spa. The Wormhole Ranch, specializing in space travel facials. You could give aromatherapy sessions, too."

"Maybe," Maria said. "Although I wouldn't mind keeping the wormhole as my personal beauty secret. And yours, I guess." She snorted as she pulled into the Crashdown's parking lot. "Like you need it. Look at you. It's no wonder you ended up with the perfect boyfriend."

My amazing boyfriend who practically goes into a coma while we're kissing, Liz thought, climbing out of the car. "Well, Michael's brother is up for grabs," she commented.

"Yeah, if I can't have the real thing, why not take the fat-free version?" Maria joked. They headed toward the restaurant.

"Next time I see Michael, I'm telling him you think he's fat," Liz teased. She pushed open the door, and the first few bars of the *Close Encounters* theme played. But the sound was almost obscured by the music coming out of her papa's office.

"Oh no." Maria gasped. "That's The Doors, isn't it? Are we late?"

Liz checked her watch. "Not late enough." Her papa only played The Doors when he was in a heinously bad mood. So whatever had his boxers in a bunch was big.

Before she and Maria were halfway to the counter, her papa burst out of his office. No, not big, she realized when she saw his face. Make that enormous. Make that nuclear.

You'd think that a guy who walked around in Grateful Dead T-shirts with his hair in a ponytail would be laid-back. But no. Liz's father had a quick temper—and he wasn't afraid to show it.

"Your mother came in for lunch today," Mr. Ortecho

told Maria as she and Liz headed toward the storage room in back that doubled as a changing room.

"Uh, that's nice," Maria said nervously. She stopped in front of him, shifting from one foot to the other.

Liz wondered if Maria was nervous because the throbbing vein in her papa's temple looked like it was about to erupt or if she was nervous because she'd figured out the same thing Liz had—Liz's father had found out that their weekend trip to the Carlsbad Caverns had been completely adult-free.

Mr. Ortecho took a step toward Maria. Maria backed a step away.

"She said it was so nice of me to take you two and your friends to the Caverns," he continued.

I got it in one, Liz thought. What am I going to say to him? It's not like I can say that I absolutely had to go to the Caverns to try and bring Alex back home from another planet.

"Which means you both lied to me and to her," Mr. Ortecho said.

"We really needed to—," Maria began, taking another step back.

"Enough," Mr. Ortecho barked. "There's no excuse for what you did, and I don't want to listen to you try to come up with one." He turned his full attention on Liz, his eyes glittering dangerously. "What I want to know is what else you've been lying about."

Liz glanced behind her at the dining room. At least the only customer was Mr. Orndorff, and he probably had his hearing aid turned off.

"Nothing," Liz promised him. It wasn't completely true, but it was mainly true. Yes, there had been other nights that she'd had to lie about where she'd been, like the night they drove to Albuquerque to get Isabel and Adam away from DuPris. But she'd never been doing any of the things she knew her papa was worried about her doing—like drinking, like drugs, like following in her sister Rosa's footsteps.

"And I'm supposed to believe this? I'm supposed to believe that I just happened to find out about the one lie you've ever told me?" Her papa's brown eyes seemed to turn darker as he spoke, darker and colder.

Liz felt something harden inside her. She straightened her spine and met her father's gaze without flinching.

"You're supposed to trust me," she answered.

He shot out one hand, grabbed her arm, and flipped it over. He studied it briefly, then checked the other one.

Needle marks. That was what he was looking for.

Liz felt like her heart had started pumping ice water instead of blood, coldness traveling down her arms and legs, up her neck and into her face.

"I have to change." She pushed her way past her papa, Maria scurrying behind her.

"I'm not through with you," he insisted.

"I have to change," Liz repeated, without turning around. If she looked at him right now, she was afraid she might hate him for the rest of her life.

"Fine. Go change," he called after her. "But from now on you're at school or here or home. No exceptions. If you need to go to the library, your mama or I will go with you."

Liz ducked into the changing room and sank down on one of the spindly chairs. She didn't think her legs would have held her up another second. Too cold.

Maria shut the door behind them, blocking out the curious, sympathetic looks from the other employees.

"You okay?"

Liz shook her head. "You know he was checking for track marks, right?"

"Yeah," Maria said softly. "Liz, you know he's just afraid because of what—"

"Because of what happened to Rosa. Because she overdosed and he feels like it's his fault for not seeing it coming," Liz finished in a singsong voice. "But you know what, Maria? I'm not my sister. And I've spent half my life trying to prove that to him and Mama."

She felt a deep, shuddering sob build up inside her, but she wasn't going to let herself cry. Not now. Not where he could hear her.

Maria sat down next to Liz and nudged her with her shoulder. "You ever think of saying to your dad what you just said to me?"

"Are you kidding?" Liz pressed her hands between her knees, trying to get her fingers warm. It didn't help. "How could I when no one in my house ever says the name Rosa? We don't even have any pictures of her anywhere. Not in the albums, not on the fridge, not in the hall. They all disappeared the day after she died. I don't know where they are. I've looked for them a bunch of times, but—"

A sharp knock on the door interrupted her. "Are you two working today, or should I be giving Evie and Jose overtime?" Liz's papa demanded.

"One minute," Maria called back. She jumped up and pulled her uniform down from the little clothes rack. Then she grabbed Liz's and held it out to her.

Liz just stared at it.

Maria gave it a shake. "Please? For me?"

"You know what I just realized?" Liz asked. "He's my father. We live in the same house. I work at his restaurant. And he doesn't even know me."

"I want to know all about you," Michael told Trevor. It came out sounding a lot dorkier than it had in his mind. He was just stupid with happiness right now. He actually had a brother!

"Like what?" Trevor asked. His head swiveled

back and forth as they walked down Roswell's main street. He obviously wanted to see *everything*.

"Like the Kindred. Is it all people who wanted the right to have more than one birthing cycle?" Michael asked.

"Some of them are," Trevor answered. "But they aren't the only ones who have to go into hiding to live the kind of life they choose."

"Really?" Michael had always pictured his home planet as this totally perfect place, a place where Michael would have this totally perfect life if he could just find his parents' ship and get there.

He realized now that was totally childish. Why would earth be the only planet in the universe where things were messed up?

"That kind of looks like your friend Alex," Trevor said, pointing at the plastic Ronald in front of McDonald's.

Alex again. This was about the fifth time Trevor had brought up Alex today.

Michael gave the plastic Ronald a fast look. "Maybe the hair, a little. Why else do people join the Kindred?" he asked, trying to change the subject.

"Some because—"

Trevor was interrupted by the toot of a car horn. Michael glanced over and saw Mrs. Pascal hanging out the window. "Michael, I want you to come over for dinner some night. We miss you. And I know Dylan would love to see you."

"Okay, I will," he called back. And he actually meant it. Mrs. Pascal seemed much less annoying when he didn't have to live with her.

"Who was that?" Trevor asked after Mrs. Pascal had driven on.

"She was one of my foster moms," Michael answered.

"How many did you have?" Trevor stopped in front of the car wash and studied the painting of a cat that was getting its spaceship polished up. "That thing could never fly," he said.

"That thing could never fly it," Michael said, nodding toward the cat.

"So how many foster moms?" Trevor asked as they continued down the street.

"Too many. I tried not to count," Michael admitted. "Did you stay with one family when you were with the Kindred?"

"No. I sort of belonged to everyone," Trevor said.

Basically the opposite of me, Michael thought. He hadn't belonged to anyone.

Michael felt a stab of disgust. Get over yourself. Like Trevor had it easy. His parents told him they would come back for him, and then he never saw them again.

"I bet Alex's parents were concerned when he disappeared," Trevor commented.

And we're back to Alex again, Michael thought. "They were completely freaked."

"There were definitely people on our planet who were concerned when he arrived." Trevor shoved his fingers through his hair, and Michael was struck by the fact that his hands and Trevor's were almost exactly the same shape and size. He wondered if that meant he and Trevor would look sort of alike in all their bodies' adaptive forms.

"Max kept trying to send the beings of the consciousness info about Alex to try to keep the freaking to a minimum," Michael said.

"What kind of stuff?" Trevor asked.

"Like how Alex helped save our butts when Sheriff Valenti, the Clean Slate agent I told you about, was zeroing in on me and Max and Isabel," Michael answered. "And how he sat with Isabel practically every second for days after the sheriff killed her boyfriend."

"Alex sounds like a good guy," Trevor commented.

"The best," Michael answered. He noticed that his mouth felt really watery, and he laughed. "I start salivating as soon as I get on this block," he told Trevor. "Come on. It's way past time for you to have your first cruller."

Michael led the way into the doughnut shop and ordered four crullers. He shoved two of them at Trevor after they sat down at one of the little tables in the back. Trevor picked one up and started to take a bite.

"Wait! Not like that!" Michael exclaimed. He

jerked Trevor's hand away from his mouth. "You've got to have hot sauce," he explained. He pulled out a handful of packets from his pocket, then he ripped a couple open and squirted them on Trevor's cruller. "Okay, now you can eat it."

Michael watched Trevor as he chewed. He smiled when he saw the awe appear on Trevor's face. "Good?"

"Amazing. Fantastic. Phenomenal," Trevor answered.

"I guess we must have the same taste buds," Michael said. He felt the little pop of pleasure he got every time he discovered a similarity between him and Trevor.

"Definitely," Trevor mumbled, his mouth full with a massive bite of cruller. "I guess Alex wouldn't go for this combo, huh?"

What's with all the questions about Alex? Michael wondered. He gave a mental shrug. He really didn't care what they talked about. He was hanging out with his brother.

# SIX

"I got the most brilliant idea last night!" Stacey Scheinin cried. "At halftime we should spell out our team's name with our bodies! Can I hear a yeah?"

All the Stacey wanna-bes immediately screamed, "Yeah."

"Sounds fabulous," Isabel added.

Everyone on the cheerleading squad stared at her. It took Isabel a moment to figure out why. Oh, she realized. It's the first time I ever agreed with Stacey about anything.

That just showed what an incredible mood she was in. She had fuzzy-wuzzy feelings toward everyone in the whole world, even look-at-how-cute-I-am, aren't-I-the-best-little-head-cheerleader-ever Stacey.

"Are you feeling okay? Because I'm suddenly in need of a barf bag," Isabel's friend Tish Okabe whispered in Isabel's ear.

"I'm feeling spectacular," Isabel answered.

Alex was back! Michael had a brother! And Sheriff Valenti was still dead!

Yeah, Elsevan DuPris was out there somewhere,

but she wasn't going to ruin one of her best days ever thinking about that.

"You're awfully happy today," Stacey said, sounding suspicious, or at least as suspicious as someone with a Minnie Mouse voice could sound. She shot a sly look over at the bleachers. "The new boy must be good for you."

Isabel followed Stacey's gaze and saw Kyle Valenti staring at her. As she watched, he pulled out a lighter and flicked it on and off, on and off.

What a loser, Isabel thought. Does he think he's at a concert or something? She felt a tiny bit of her joy drain away. Little Kyle clearly had something on his mind. Something vicious.

Deliberately she turned her back on him. Kyle was an insect. When he became annoying enough, she would deal with him. "Some of my fans do get a little overadoring," Isabel told Stacey.

"I bet you're sorry you jettisoned Alex," Lucinda Baker called out. "I saw him bending over the drinking fountain. He's been doing his butt-building exercises, that's all I can say."

"Uh-*huh*," one of the Stacey wanna-bes added. "I can't believe I never noticed how yummy he is."

Alex had definitely come back home with something different about him. He'd been weak and scared, yeah. But when Isabel finally got used to the fact that he was really and truly home, she couldn't help notice that he'd undergone some

78

kind of transformation. It was like he had a glow about him. But she wasn't going to stand around and discuss that with the squad.

"So do you want to practice the letter thing now?" Isabel asked Stacey.

"It's getting late. We'll do it next time. That's it for today," Stacey answered. She sounded sort of confused.

I have to remember this, Isabel thought. If I want to mess with Stacey's head, all I have to do is be nice to her.

"You don't actually have something going with Kyle, do you?" Tish asked as she and Isabel headed for the locker room.

"Did I just hear you ask me if I had something going with Kyle?" Isabel asked with mock horror.

Tish grinned. "Okay, but you do have something going with somebody. I can see it on your face. So come on. Confess. Did you get back with Alex? Because he is looking extra crispy." She held the locker-room door open for Isabel, then led the way over to their lockers.

"Tish, come back from the fifties, okay?" Isabel sat down on one of the peeling wooden benches and kicked off her shoes. "A guy is not the only reason for a girl to be happy."

Although she had to admit that Trevor had . . . possibilities.

"Don't even try giving me that superior attitude,"

Tish answered. "I know exactly how many times you saw the last Julia Roberts movie, okay?"

"I'm not saying I don't like guys," Isabel answered. "Guys can be very entertaining. I'm just saying there are other things in life."

She opened her locker and reached for her towel. She always brought her own. The ones at school were way too thin. Plus other people used them.

When she pulled the towel free, a doll fell to the floor with a soft plop.

"What a cute little cheerleader outfit it has on," Tish cooed. She picked it up, and Isabel saw the doll's face for the first time.

Make that the glob of charred plastic where the doll's face used to be.

Kyle and his lighter have been busy, Isabel thought. She took the doll from Tish and used the very tips of her fingers to deposit it in the trash. Now she really couldn't wait to get into the shower.

I suppose I should deal with that boy sooner rather than later, she thought.


"You're in trouble," Kevin said with a smirk.

Maria shut the door behind her. "Don't sound so happy about it," she answered. "Remember how many things I know about you—things that Mom would be very interested in, things that could put you in your room for life."

80

"I'm so scared." Kevin gave an exaggerated shiver that made his arms flop around like over-cooked spaghetti.

"Maria, is that you?" her mother called from the kitchen.

"Yeah," she called back.

"Come in here for a minute," her mom answered.

"See?" Kevin mouthed.

Maria ignored her little brother and headed toward the kitchen. At least there is no way this will even get close to the meltdown between Liz and her dad, she thought. She took a deep breath and stepped through the door.

Her eyes immediately went to the mosaic of miniature candy bars laid out on the table in front of her mom. Uh-oh. Bad sign. Maria's mom stayed away from candy except when she was in major stress mode.

"I heard from Mr. Ortecho that your trip to the caverns was unchaperoned," her mother said.

*Unchaperoned.* What a weird, old-fashioned word. Like they should have taken a prim governess in a long black dress with them. The thought brought a giggle bubbling up Maria's throat. She covered it with a cough. Laughing right now would not help the situation.

"Yeah," Maria admitted. "But I didn't really *say* Mr. Ortecho would be with us. You just interpreted—"

"Maria."

81

That one word, in that tone of voice, was enough to make Maria give up her feeble attempt at coming up with an excuse.

Her mother unwrapped one of the little candy bars and popped the whole thing in her mouth.

"Maria," she repeated, her voice softer now, more tentative. She peeled another candy bar, popped it. "Maria, have you . . . ? Are you . . . ?"

She reached for another piece of candy. Maria pinned her hand to the table, stopping her.

"I have to say, I have no idea what you're attempting to communicate here," she told her mom.

"I'm so bad at this," her mother burst out. "I've spent half the day trying to figure out how to talk to you about, um, intimacy."

Intimacy, Maria silently repeated.

Oh no. Oh. My. God! Her mother wanted to have a sex talk!

Maria grabbed one of the candy bars, unwrapped it, and shoved it in her mouth. Two refined-sugar intakes in one week. What was wrong with her?

"I'm not happy that you spent the weekend alone with some boys," her mother said. She pulled her hand free of Maria's but left the candy on the table. "But I know that—that sex isn't something that can only happen on a weekend away from home."

She had started sounding somewhat robotic. Maria figured this must be the beginning of her prepared speech.

"Mom, you don't have to. I'm not . . . I haven't. It's not an issue," Maria stammered.

But her mother was unstoppable. "The most important thing to me is that you're safe. Now, we can make you an appointment with my gynecologist and get you a prescription for the pill. But as I hope you know, that won't protect you against AIDS or venere—"

"Mom, believe me, there's no one I'm interested in . . . being with," Maria insisted.

Except Michael, she added to herself. And there's no possibility of anything intimate happening between us. Not when he's still wrecked by Cameron leaving. Not when I'm going nuts pretending I'm just his buddy.

"All right, I'll only say one more thing." Her mother started to put the remaining candy bars back in the bag. "Wait for someone you really care about, who really cares about you."

Michael. It was him or nobody.

Maria's heart tightened in her chest. She could be facing a very, very long wait. Like forever.

"I promise," Maria told her mother. "But you really don't—"

The phone began to ring, interrupting her. Maria tipped her chair back far enough to grab the receiver. "Hello?"

"I can see you right now," a male voice said. "Sitting at the kitchen table with your mother.

Having a little heart-to-heart. It's very sweet."

Maria opened her mouth, but she couldn't get any words out. Her throat was too dry.

"I can see your brother, too," the voice continued. "In the living room, playing some video game. Yes, I can see everybody in the house, every move they make."

There was a click, and the dial tone started to hum in her ear.

"Who was it?" Maria's mother asked.

Maria swallowed hard. "Wrong number," she answered. She stood up and crossed to the kitchen window. The front yard was dark and empty. So were the sidewalk and the street.

But Maria knew someone was close by. Watching. She pulled the curtains closed.

It's just Kyle, she told herself. It has to be just Kyle, right?

But even if it is just Kyle, she thought, a tingle of uneasiness running down her spine, what if he gets tired of just watching?

Alex slid into bed, his own bed, with the dip in the middle that fit his body perfectly. I'm home, he thought for probably the fifty-second time that day.

He didn't expect to be able to sleep—at least not right away. He figured his brain was crammed with way too much info—about his dad and Trevor, mainly. But when Alex's head sank down into his soft, goose-down pillow and he closed his eyes, he immediately felt that slipping-sliding wooziness he always got when he was just about to go under.

The next thing he knew, he was falling. No, not falling, being hurled—down, down, down. His velocity pushed the flesh of his cheeks back toward his ears, curled his top lip toward his nose.

Alex clawed at the air, grasping for something to stop him. But there was nothing but the void all around him as he flew down, faster and faster.

He could feel the pressure building internally. His bladder and stomach felt weighted down. Each beat of his heart seemed to take massive effort, as did each breath he pulled into his burning lungs.

He was in a wormhole.

You're dreaming, Alex told himself. You're home in bed.

But the thought didn't jar him awake.

He felt suction coming from behind him, pulling him backward. But the other force was still hurtling him straight down.

Alex heard his bones creak as his body stretched out, thrown forward and hauled back simultaneously. A gash opened up on his stomach. He felt a rush of hot blood. Then a matching gash opened on his back.

He was being ripped apart. And he was powerless to stop it.

He opened his mouth and screamed. Then his whole body jerked, and he sat up fast—hyperawake.

His heart was pounding so hard, he could feel the beats in his throat and ears and temples. He lowered himself back down. The sheet under his back was damp with sweat.

He hoped he hadn't screamed out loud. His little talk with the Major had been very cool. He didn't want the good feeling between them to evaporate because he'd woken up hollering like a baby.

You're in your room. You're safe. Your body's still in one piece. Just get a grip, he ordered himself. His heartbeat slowed down a little. But when his eyes adjusted to the darkness, it kicked right back into high gear.

He wasn't alone. Someone stood in the shadows near his dresser.

Alex slowly, shakily slipped his hand out of the covers. He reached under the bed, feeling for his Louisville slugger, keeping his eyes locked on the motionless figure. After he wrapped his fingers around the bat's smooth wooden handle, he tensed his muscles, preparing himself to spring.

But suddenly the intruder was gone.

Not out the door. Not out the window. Just gone.

It had to be Trevor, he thought. When he saw that *I* saw him, he teleported out of here.

Alex jumped out of bed. Did Trevor get the Stone?

He clicked on the overhead light and grabbed the peanut butter jar filled with marbles off his dresser. He dumped the marbles onto his bed, cursing as a bunch of them hit the floor.

Was it there? Was it? His fingers flew over the marbles, sorting, sorting.

Got it. Thank you, Edgar Allan Poe, he thought. When he was eleven, he'd read all the guy's stories about twenty times each. *The Purloined Letter* had given him the idea for hiding the Stone pretty much in plain sight.

But a good hiding place wouldn't stop Trevor next time. Alex was sure he'd come after the Stone again. And the Louisville wouldn't have much of a chance against Trevor's powers.

# SEVEN

"This is the first party I've ever thrown," Michael told Adam and Trevor. "The place is getting trashed again." But he smiled. The museum was the perfect party space, and everyone from school was taking full advantage.

Half of Isabel's cheerleading squad was holding court in the coffee shop in the back. Over by the Elvis on Mars display there was already some dancing going on that was a lot more like making out.

"Why the first?" Trevor asked. He took a swig of his Lime Warp, grimaced, and set the can on the floor.

"Michael and I haven't lived here that long," Adam answered quickly. Michael got the feeling he was a little jealous of Trevor. He could understand that. Michael was sort of like Adam's big brother/roommate. And now Michael's *real* brother had shown up—and moved in.

"And before I lived here, it was all foster homes—which are never exactly party central," Michael said. "But anyway, this is the optimum night for a party. No one's sick. No one's locked in the compound." He slapped Adam on the shoulder, and Adam flashed his eager puppy-dog smile. "No one's on another planet. No one's trying to kill us, at least not right this second. And—"

"Oh no, no, no," Maria cried as she squeezed her way between Michael and Trevor. "There's going to be no talk about killing tonight. It's Alex and Trevor's welcome-home slash welcome-to-earth party."

"So what *should* we talk about?" Michael asked her.

"Little fuzzy bunnies with little pink noses," Maria answered immediately. "Little fuzzy bunny slippers with little pink noses would also be acceptable."

Michael cracked up. He never knew what was going to come spilling out of Maria's raspberry-colored mouth. "How about the fact that your little brother is attempting to see up Kieran Scott's dress as we speak?"

Maria let out a yelp. She started toward Kevin, but Michael blocked her way.

"I think Max has it covered," he told her. He glanced over his shoulder just to make sure and saw Max leading Kevin over to the office, where Ray had set up an assortment of old pinball machines.

"Sorry I had to bring him," Maria said. "Mom couldn't find a baby-sitter. She's going to pick him up in about half an hour."

"Not a problem," Michael answered.

"So if we'd grown up here together, is that what I'd have had to do with you?" Trevor asked. He raised an eyebrow at Michael. "Take you to parties that I didn't want you at in the first place?"

Michael could hardly imagine what his life would have been like if Trevor had been around. Everything would have been radically different. Even if they'd been in foster homes, at least they would have had each other.

"You're not that much older than me," Michael reminded him, clamping down on the sentimental trash in his head. "I probably would have gotten invited to all the cool parties and had to take *you* along."

"Would not," Trevor countered.

"Would too," Michael joked.

Maria laughed. "You really are brothers, aren't you?"

"Definitely," Trevor answered. "I paid special attention to all the materials the Kindred gave me on sibling relationships. I wanted to make sure I treated Michael right." He reached over and socked Michael on the arm. "Is that right? Or should I be giving you a wedgie?"

Michael felt himself starting to grin like an idiot and tried to get a grip.

"What I studied didn't mention that friends take responsibility for their friends' siblings," Trevor added.

"You lost me," Michael admitted. He drained his soda in a long gulp.

"The way that Max took charge of Kevin just

now," Trevor explained, jerking his chin toward the office.

"That's not so usual," Maria told him. "It's just that in our group, we're almost more like family than friends. I guess that makes Kevin kind of an honorary little brother to Max."

"I definitely think of him as my little brother," Adam volunteered.

As far as Michael knew, this party was only the second time Adam had ever seen Kevin. But Michael wasn't about to bring that up. Not when Adam was trying so hard to prove he was one of them.

"So, okay, you guys. Back to the important topic of bunny's noses. Adam, what color pink would you say they are?" Maria joked.

"You have to tell me what you're on," Michael teased. "I want to be sure to avoid it."

Maria tilted back her head and stared him in the eye. "Just a little tangerine oil, which is very invigorating," she answered, all serious.

"Can I have some?" Trevor asked.

"Of course." Maria opened her ridiculously small purse and pulled out a vial of oil. She took out the stopper, dabbed some of the oil on her fingers, and then rubbed it into the base of Trevor's throat.

"You could have just given him the vial," Michael muttered. He wanted Trevor to experience pretty much all the cool things earth had to offer— but not getting touched by Maria.

"It's better if it's on a pulse point," Maria explained, still smoothing the oil into Trevor's skin.

"Feels good to me," Trevor answered. He pressed her fingers back to his throat when she started to pull them away.

Michael felt his face start to flush. Was Trevor hitting on Maria? Exactly what "local behavioral norms" had he learned before he showed up here?

"Feels good to me, too," Maria told him. "Did you know fat-free cookies can taste amazingly like the fat-full ones?"

Was *she* hitting on Trevor? That oil was long gone, and she still hadn't taken her hand away. Michael narrowed his eyes, studying her. Maria's aura was sparkling, little silver flecks scattered through the silky blue.

Michael shoved his hands through his hair. Yeah, there was a very real possibility that she was flirting. He shot another glance at her. Make that she was definitely flirting.

"I've never had a fat-free cookie," Trevor answered, smiling down at Maria.

"Don't listen to her. She doesn't know anything about cookies. She doesn't even eat cookies," Michael informed him.

"I might start," Maria said, still looking at Trevor. Although Michael thought he caught her giving him a lightning-fast glance out of the corner of her eye.

Is she *trying* to make me crazy?

"So, Trevor, what do you—," Maria began.

Then the lights flickered and the crowd gave an oooh of anticipation. "Get ready to bop!" someone shouted.

"Give me a friggin' break," Michael muttered. He took a step toward the guy manning the big boom box, but Maria snagged him by the elbow.

"Come on, Michael. We have to give Trevor and Adam the chance to experience the bop," she said.

Michael groaned. But he knew Maria well enough to know that she'd be relentless until she got what she wanted.

"There wasn't anything about the bunny hop in the material you studied, was there?" he asked Trevor as the bop music started to blare.

Trevor nodded, glancing around at the lines of people starting to form up and down the aisles of the museum. "Bunny hop, Charleston, swing dancing, disco, break dancing, everything," he answered.

"You swing dance?" Maria exclaimed. "I would love to learn that."

"One of the guards taught me the bunny hop," Adam volunteered loudly, clearly feeling a little left out again.

"Okay, well, both of you should know that Roswell has its own special version of the bunny hop called the alien bop," Michael explained. "It's about to start, so be afraid, be very afraid."

"There's nothing to be afraid of," Maria said.

"Except looking like a dork," Michael interrupted.

She ignored him, focusing on Adam and Trevor. "What you do is, you put your arms around the waist of the person in front of you." She moved up behind Michael to illustrate, standing close enough that her breasts brushed lightly against him.

Suddenly Michael didn't think the bop was such a horrible idea. Especially since Maria was demonstrating on him and not Trevor.

"Then you kind of bend your knee one way while you twist your foot the other way," Michael said, looking from Trevor to Adam.

"Excellent party!" Maggie McMahon called as she bopped past, followed by her boyfriend, who was dressed in a guy version of the outfit Maggie was wearing. Pathetic.

"Would I give any other kind?" Michael shouted back.

"What do we do after the leg-bending thing?" Adam asked.

"You know what? It's easier if you just watch everyone else and imitate what they do." Michael grabbed Adam by the back of the shirt.

"Now, you grab onto Trevor," he said, before Trevor could wrap his arms around Maria.

Adam obediently linked his fingers through Trevor's belt loops. "Now what?"

"Now we bop!" Maria shouted.

\*        \*        \*

Isabel sat at the top of the spiral staircase, staring down at the party happening below. She liked being able to see everyone in her little group at once, well, everyone but Liz, who was practically being held prisoner at home. Somehow it made her feel safe to see them all together, and safe wasn't something she'd had enough of in her life.

Her eyes ran from person to person—Michael and Trevor scarfing pizza with sugar off one of the display cases, Adam stretched out on the floor with his head next to the boom box, Maria saying something to Max that was making him laugh by the front window, and Alex getting hit on by Stacey Scheinin near the entrance to the coffee shop.

Wait . . . what?

"Uh-uh. Not gonna happen, Stacey," Isabel whispered. She leaped to her feet and rushed down the stairs. Then she slowed down and casually made her way over to Stacey and Alex.

She could see why Stacey's guy antennae had led her in Alex's direction. There was something different about Alex since he got back. It was like he was giving off a double dose of those pheromones that caused sexual attraction or something. He'd been getting looks from practically every girl in the place.

And that was fine. Good for Alex. Really. But Stacey was not getting her Princess Pink nails into him. She'd said way too many nasty things behind Alex's back in the past.

"Sorry, Stacey, I have to borrow Alex from you," she said sweetly. She took Alex by the hand and pulled him over to the improvised dance floor that had been made by shoving a bunch of display cases against the wall.

"Isabel, you know when you break up with someone, you can't get pissed if they talk to another girl at a party," Alex said, but he didn't sound mad. He pulled her close as a slow song started to play.

"I know," she answered, not bothering to explain that he could do way better. She didn't feel like talking right now, especially about Stacey.

She rested her head on Alex's shoulder and let herself completely absorb the fact that he was home. She wondered if she'd ever find anything that felt better than this.

"What do you think of Trevor?" Alex asked.

"I'm happy for Michael," Isabel murmured.

"That's not what I asked," Alex said.

Isabel lifted her head so she could look at him. The muscles in his jaw were tight, and the expression in his green eyes was intense and challenging.

She gave a mental sigh. Was this some kind of jealousy issue? This was Alex's first night out since he came back. She didn't want to have to sit him down and have some kind of it's-going-to-be-weird-seeing-each-other-with-new-people-but-it's-got-to-happen speech.

"What do *you* think of Trevor?" she asked, deciding that was the easiest way to go.

"I think none of us really knows him yet," Alex said slowly. "I think until we do, we should be . . . cautious."

And I think Alex *is* getting a case of the jealous, Isabel decided. But she wasn't going to let that ruin the night for any of them. She snuggled up closer to Alex and rested her cheek against his chest.

"Cautious. That makes sense," she mumbled.

To her relief, Alex didn't say anything else. They just danced. When the song ended, Isabel kept her arms around Alex. He tightened his grip on her, burying his face in the side of her neck. Then he slowly pulled away. "Thanks for the dance," he said, his green eyes warm as he looked at her.

Isabel had the feeling Alex was talking about more than the dance, that he was talking about their whole horrible/wonderful time together as a couple. She reached out and ran her hand down his cheek.

"Thank *you*."

They stared at each other for a long moment, then they each seemed to realize there was nothing else to say. Something was ending, and they had to let it happen.

Isabel gave Alex a last smile. She turned around and pushed her way through the crowd, heading back toward her perch on the staircase. Then she stopped. She didn't feel like just watching anymore. She didn't feel like just being safe.

Besides, she was Isabel Evans. And that carried responsibilities. She had to let everyone at the party see how fabulous she looked tonight. It's not like she'd bought her form-hugging pink dress so no one would notice her.

Tish Okabe waved to her from the other side of the room, and Isabel started toward her. Then she felt a hand on her shoulder. She glanced back and saw Trevor. "Would you want to dance with me?" he asked.

"Of course," Isabel answered. "You should know that every girl in the place would want to dance with you. Your earth adaptation is definitely yummy."

"Yummy?" Trevor repeated.

"As in I've got to get me a taste of that," Isabel teased. She slid her arms around his neck, and after a moment's hesitation Trevor positioned his hands at her waist.

The feel of his hands reminded her of Michael. Trevor's gray eyes reminded her of Michael, too. But Trevor's hands, Trevor's eyes . . . they did something to her that Michael's didn't, making her body feel almost liquid.

"You two know this is a fast song, right?" Isabel heard Maria call. She twirled past them, with Adam trailing behind her.

She's right, Isabel realized with a start. It was as if when she looked at Trevor, everything had slowed down. Reluctantly she released him and got herself moving to the music that was actually playing.

"I wasn't trying to get you to stop," Maria said. Isabel spun toward her, and the two of them started dancing face-to-face, ignoring the guys.

"Not a problem," Isabel answered. She was almost glad to be free of Trevor's touch. It had been almost too intense. Maybe Alex was right to warn her about him. She had the feeling if he got too close, he could melt her into a little puddle on the floor. Had he felt anything even close to what she had?

Isabel shook her head, realizing she'd never wondered that about a guy before.

"What?" Maria asked.

"Nothing," Isabel called back. She felt someone grab her hand, and she was pulled into a spin.

"Hey, I was dancing with Maria," Isabel told Michael when she realized it was him who'd snagged her.

"And now you're dancing with me," Michael announced.

"I guess I'll have to make do with Alex," Maria said. She crooked her finger at him, and he danced his way over to her.

Isabel caught him giving Trevor a hard, evaluating look. Trevor noticed. He gave Alex the same stare right back. Not tonight, boys, she thought.

"I saw you making goo-goo eyes at my brother," Michael told Isabel, pulling her attention back to him. She could hear the pride in his voice when he said the word *brother*.

"So what if I was?" Isabel asked. But she didn't like the idea that she'd been so obvious. Obvious wasn't her style.

"I guess he's a good substitute if you can't have me," Michael teased. He dipped her, a big, dramatic dip that had the ends of her hair brushing the floor.

Isabel looked up and saw Adam staring down at her, laughing. She hauled herself back up, using Michael's arm for leverage. Then she reached over, took Adam by one shoulder and one hand, and tried to dip him. They both would have landed on the floor if Michael and Trevor hadn't steadied them.

This is the way it should always be, she thought. All of us together. Then she glanced around, realizing someone was missing.

Where was Max?

"Max, come dance with us!" Isabel shouted.

"In a minute," he called back. "I promised I'd call Liz and give her a live report from the party."

"Tell her we miss her," Maria called.

Max nodded, then wove his way through the crowd and over to the spiral staircase. He took the steps two at a time. The apartment was empty except for a couple making out on Adam's air mattress. Max ignored them. It wasn't like they'd be listening in on his conversation. He could set off a grenade in here and they wouldn't notice.

He headed for a phone in the kitchen, then paused as he got a flicker of interest from the consciousness. He deepened his connection slightly, and a group of the beings began pulsing with the rhythm of the music from the party, their pleasure almost transcendent.

Max sank down to the floor and leaned his head against the wall, deepening the connection even further until he felt the pulsing begin in his own body and the explosions of pure glee go off in his head.

"Max, I need to talk to you." Alex's voice sounded so far away, almost inaudible under the music. The music. The music that felt more a part of Max than his own heartbeat.

"Now, Max," Alex insisted.

Reluctantly Max turned down the volume on his connection to the consciousness, and the music began to sound ordinary again.

But it was a different song than when he came upstairs, he realized. And the couple on the air mattress had disappeared.

"How long have I been up here?" he muttered.

"At least an hour," Alex answered. He sat down next to Max. "There's something I've got to tell you. I should have told you before, but I, stupidly, wanted to wait and try to get more info first."

Max felt his muscles tighten when he took in the splotches of gray in Alex's aura. "So what's the deal? Or should we get the others before you start?"

Alex shook his head. "I was actually waiting until I had a chance to talk to you alone," he admitted. Then he reached into his pocket and pulled out a small, opalescent stone that shone with a blue-green light.

A shudder ran through Max's body as a burst of joy and loss from the consciousness exploded inside him. "It's another one of the Stones of Midnight," he whispered.

"Yeah. This is what gave me the power to come through the wormhole." Alex hesitated for a second, clenching his fist tight around the Stone, then rushed on. "I don't think Trevor came to earth to have some family reunion with Michael. I think he came for the Stone. And I think he would have killed me to get it."

Max's first thought was for Michael. If what Alex said was true, it would rip Michael apart.

"Wait—what makes you think it was Trevor?" Max demanded. "You didn't actually *see* him or anything, did you? Couldn't there have been a third being in the wormhole?"

Alex closed his eyes and rubbed them with his free hand. "Yeah, I guess it's possible."

He opened his eyes, the gray spots in his aura darkening until they were almost black.

"But Max, when I'm near Trevor, I get scared. I feel like an idiot admitting it. But it's the truth. I get this physical fear response, and I'm sure it's because I'm picking up all these subtle, subliminal clues that Trevor is the one who was trying to kill me that night."

Yellow lines of fear snaked across Alex's aura. Just talking about Trevor freaks Alex out, Max realized. And Alex didn't freak out all that easily.

"I was thinking maybe you could try and get some background on Trevor from the consciousness," Alex continued.

"Maybe," Max answered. "I mean, it's not like I can type in his name and get a bio, but I might be able to get something. And I'd rather not talk to Michael until—"

"That's one of the reasons I wanted to talk to you alone," Alex agreed. "And I thought you should be the one to have this."

Alex gently placed the Stone in Max's hand. Max could feel the power churning under its smooth surface.

"Okay, just give me a minute." Max closed his eyes and let his connection to the consciousness deepen until he almost couldn't tell where he left off and the other beings began. He formed an image of Trevor and sent it out in a wave that he hoped would ripple all the way through the ocean of auras.

Almost immediately the auras around him began to vibrate. Their hues changed rapidly in a cacophony of color that burned Max's eyes. Then the changes slowed down as all the auras got closer and closer to the same shade.

Red. The vivid bloodred of pure fury.

Max didn't know what the deal was exactly, but he knew that the rage was directed at Trevor.

And he knew that the consciousness believed Trevor was a danger to Max. To all of them.

# EIGHT

"I can see you're having a wild Saturday night," the scruffy twenty-something guy behind the counter of the minimart said. He dropped the bottle of vanilla in a little brown bag and handed Liz her change.

Oh, great, she thought. You know your life has hit a new low when the minimart guy finds you pathetic.

"I'm just about to head over to a party my friends are giving at the UFO museum," Liz lied.

The guy gave her a knowing smile, and Liz felt her face get hot.

She didn't think there was any lower she could sink, but it turned out there was—trying to convince the minimart guy you had a life. And failing.

"Thanks," she muttered. She snatched up her bag and got out of the place as fast as she could.

But as soon as she was clear of the guy's sight, she slowed down. She was in no hurry to get home.

I wonder if Max will have called while I was gone, she thought. She'd expected him to call hours ago, but nothing. Like it would have killed him to tear himself away from the party for a few minutes?

Liz knew she had entered the self-pity zone, but she just didn't care. She figured she should just move in—pitch a tent or something. It wasn't like her life was going to get better anytime soon.

She turned onto her street. When she saw the porch light on at her house, she tried to remember if she'd flipped on the light when she left. She didn't think so.

Just as Liz reached the sidewalk, her front door swung open. Her papa stood there, glaring at her. His arms were folded across his chest, blocking out most of the line of dancing teddy bears printed on the front of his T-shirt.

"You were told not to leave the house," he said before she was halfway across the lawn.

White-hot anger erupted inside Liz. She strode up to her father and thrust the bag into his hands so hard, he almost dropped it.

"I was out scoring some drugs," she told him. She'd never said anything like that to her papa before, but it just came spewing out. And she was glad it had.

Her father took a quick look into the bag. His grim expression didn't soften.

"That isn't funny," he snapped.

"You know what else isn't funny?" Liz demanded, taking a step closer so she was right in his face. "It isn't funny that my own father doesn't trust me enough to let me leave the house."

The front door opened again, and Liz's mama appeared. "I asked Liz to go to the store for me," she said. "I forgot I didn't have enough vanilla to finish my cake, and I have to deliver it first thing in the morning."

Liz's papa jerked around to face her mother. "I don't want Liz leaving the house except for school or work unless she's with one of us," he informed her, his voice as harsh as when he'd been talking to Liz.

"All I did was—," Liz began, her anger still hotter than lava.

"Let's discuss this inside," Liz's mama interrupted. "Unless you two want to ask the neighbors for an opinion poll." She brushed distractedly at the flour covering the bib of her well-worn overalls as she led the way inside.

"There's nothing to discuss." But Mr. Ortecho followed his wife into the house. Liz took a deep breath, trying to get some kind of control over her temper, and headed after them.

"I agree that Liz should be punished for lying to us about the trip to the caverns," Mrs. Ortecho said as she closed the door.

"Of course she should be punished!" Liz's papa exploded.

The foyer was small, and his angry voice bounced off the walls. Liz felt bombarded, as if his words had physical weight.

Liz's mother made little patting, smoothing gestures in the air, as if she were trying to shape a loaf of bread. Not going to happen, Mama, Liz thought. There's no way to turn this situation into something Martha Stewart nice and neat.

"But not to let her go to the library or the store or even for a walk seems excessive," Mrs. Ortecho continued.

"Excessive?" Liz's papa repeated. "I'm trying to save our child's life, and you call it excessive?"

Liz's mama gave a little gasp, so soft Liz almost didn't hear it. Then she turned away and started to run down the hall.

As Liz watched her mother leave, she felt something tearing inside her, something that ripped away as her mother disappeared into her bedroom.

She pressed her hands over her abdomen, as if her body had actually been torn open.

It was the first time any of the three of them had even alluded to Rosa's death, even in such a roundabout way—at least in front of each other.

"I have something to tell you, and I want you both to listen," Liz announced, her voice strong and steady. Her mama didn't open the bedroom door, but Liz knew she was listening. Liz waited until her papa locked his eyes on hers.

And then she said the thing she thought she could never say. The thing that had been eating away at her like acid for years.

"I'm not Rosa."

\*　　　\*　　　\*

"No one left but us," Michael said, looking around at his friends. He locked the museum's front door.

"Should we start cleaning now?" Maria asked, checking out the empty soda cans and pizza boxes scattered around the floor. "Or be lazy and—"

"There's something we need to talk about," Max announced, cutting her off.

The sharp edge to his voice instantly had everyone gathering around him.

"What's going on?" Michael demanded. He couldn't believe he hadn't noticed how messed up Max's aura was.

Max shoved his hands through his hair. "Here's the deal," he said, his eyes locked on Michael's. "Alex felt something follow him through the wormhole, something that wanted to kill him."

"But it turned out that he was wrong," Maria protested. "It was just Trevor." A few of the silver sparkles in Maria's aura winked out.

"Alex and I thought there might be a third being in the hole with him. He asked me if I could get some information from the consciousness."

Michael's teeth squeaked as he ground them together. He had a feeling he knew where this was going.

"I sent out sort of a feeler about Trevor because that was the starting place we had." Max jammed his hands in his pockets and glanced around the circle without actually meeting anyone's eyes.

"You did what?" Michael demanded, although Max had said what Michael had been afraid he was going to say. He shot a look at Trevor. His brother's face was impassive, his aura a perfect, even beige.

"What I got back was—," Max continued, as if Michael hadn't even said anything.

"I don't want to hear it," Michael interrupted again. "If there's anything Trevor wants us to know about him, he'll tell us himself." He glanced from Maria, to Isabel, to Adam, to Alex, looking for some backup.

"Usually I'd agree with you," Alex told him. "But not this time. All our lives could be at stake. That's why I asked Max to check Trevor out."

Michael felt like punching something. Something he could whale on until his hands were bruised and bloody, until he was so exhausted that's all he could think about.

"I can't believe you're saying this," he burst out. "You're talking about my brother."

"I realize he's your brother, but we don't really know anything about him," Max answered.

"Right, we don't know anything about him at all," Maria jumped in. "Good or bad."

But Michael noticed that she had backed up half a step away from Trevor, and he saw that threads of sickly yellow had begun twining through her aura. She was scared.

"What possible reason would Trevor have for trying to kill you?" Isabel asked Alex.

Isabel's question hadn't sounded challenging. It hadn't sounded like she was defending Trevor, either. It was more like she was staying neutral until she had all the facts.

Which was the same as siding against Michael's brother. The same as siding against Michael. Was Michael the only one who knew that there was no way his brother could be some kind of potential murderer? This was total insanity.

Michael positioned himself at Trevor's side, wanting him to know that at least Michael was with him however this thing shook down. He wished he had some clue what Trevor was thinking, but his brother still had that blank look on his face, and he hadn't said a word.

"Show them," Alex told Max.

Max reached into his pocket and pulled out a stone that was filled with a pulsing blue-green light. The glow distorted the planes of his face, making him look like a stranger to Michael.

"A Stone?" Isabel breathed.

"What does that thing prove?" Michael demanded.

Alex ignored him and nailed Trevor with a hard look. "You're not going to try to pretend you don't know what that is, are you?"

"Of course I know what it is. I doubt you could find anyone on my planet who doesn't,"

Trevor answered, his voice flat. "It's one of the Stones of Midnight." He stretched his hand toward it, then caught himself and jammed his fingers into his pocket instead.

"It's power, pure power," Isabel said. "I can see someone killing for that." Her tone was still neutral, as if she were talking about the weather or something.

Michael felt like shaking her.

"I can tell you for sure that someone was searching my room last night," Alex jumped in again. "I didn't see their face. But they teleported out, so that kind of narrows things down." He turned to Michael. "I mean, that does narrow things down, right?"

It's like he was begging Michael to understand that . . . that this wasn't personal or something. Michael looked away. He didn't know what he'd end up doing if he didn't. That I'm-sorry-but-I've-got-to-do-this expression on Alex's face was about to make Michael go ballistic.

"Max, I think we need to hear what the consciousness told you," Maria said. She shot an apologetic glance at Michael.

Oh, so she was sorry, too. Well, that made this witch-hunt just fine, didn't it? As long as everybody felt bad, it didn't matter that they were accusing Michael's brother of something heinous.

"Just as, you know, a precaution," Maria added. She bent down and picked up a soda can off the floor, then stared at it as if she'd never seen one before.

"I think you'd all be more comfortable discussing me if I wasn't here," Trevor said suddenly. Then he turned on his heel and strode toward the door.

"I'm coming with you," Michael called after him. But Max grabbed his arm before he could move.

Michael jerked his arm away. He stumbled backward, ramming into one of the glass display cases.

"I can't believe that you just did that. I can't believe that you all—" He stopped. There were no words that could explain how he felt right now. They'd all betrayed him, and they didn't even know it.

"We didn't say that Trevor had done anything wrong. We just need to talk it through," Maria said softly, talking to Michael as if he were some kind of wild animal that needed to be coaxed back into its cage.

"No!" Michael shouted. "No!" He slammed his fist down onto the case, and the top shattered. Shards of glass speared into his skin. Michael squeezed his fingers even tighter against his palm, forcing the glass in deeper, welcoming the pain.

"Let me heal that for you," Max said, in the same soft voice Maria had been using.

"I don't need anything from you," Michael shot back. He'd never thought he'd say those words to Max, Max, who'd always been there for him. But Michael meant the words, every one of them.

There was a choice to be made here, and he was

making it. He turned on his heel and started toward the door.

"Don't," Max ordered. "The consciousness said Trevor was dangerous. He could turn on you the second you're alone."

Michael shot a glance at Max over his shoulder. "You don't get it, do you?" he asked. "He's my *brother*."

He sprinted out the door into the dark night. Trevor was already more than a block away. Without hesitation Michael took off after him.

Adam swept the floor of the empty museum. He wasn't sure what he was going to do when he was finished.

Should he go look for Michael? He'd been gone for more than three hours. Adam grabbed the dustpan out of the waistband of his jeans, then pushed the pile of dirt into the pan.

I haven't felt any pain or fear or anything from Michael. Or from Trevor, Adam thought. He emptied the dustpan into the garbage can behind the information counter. So they're probably okay.

He did a scan of the museum, hoping there was some other party cleanup task to keep him busy. When his eyes passed over the big front window, he felt an itchy sensation go from the top of his neck all the way to the base of his spine. Windows still sort of gave him the creeps sometimes. Gave him that feeling of huge amounts of space out there, waiting to bear down on him.

Adam touched the sunglasses in his pocket but didn't put them on. They'd been a present from Liz when he first got out of the compound. She'd thought they'd help cut down on the bewildering and dazzling stimuli that was part of everyday life aboveground. And they'd worked. But Adam liked the dazzle, even when it made him feel a little nuts.

He put the broom and the dustpan in the little closet behind the counter, then hesitated. He couldn't shake the feeling that he should be doing something—like maybe going to talk to Max and Isabel and see if the three of them could figure out some course of action to deal with the Trevor situation. Adam figured it was better than going upstairs and sitting on his butt, just hoping everything was okay with Michael.

He hurried to the front door and realized there was someone standing on the other side. Liz.

Adam's fingers shook as he fumbled with the lock and opened the door for her. His heart contracted as he saw that her eyes were red from crying and that her aura had crimson splotches of anger almost completely obscured by a thick webbing of the dark purple that signified deep grief.

"I guess you heard about Michael and Trevor," he began.

Liz dropped a gym bag on the floor. "Do you

think I could stay here with you guys for a while? I'd go to Maria's, but I'm sure my father would find me and drag me home."

Obviously this *wasn't* about Michael and Trevor. "Of course you can stay," Adam told her. "Stay as long as you want. But Liz, what's wrong?"

"I had a fight with my papa," she answered, twisting her long dark hair into a knot on top of her head. "A fight. That sounds so minor." Her voice broke, and Adam saw fresh tears begin to fall down her cheeks. "I don't know if he'll ever talk to me again. I don't know if I'm ever going to be able to go home."

She covered her face with her hands, but she couldn't hide the fact that her shoulders were heaving with sobs, sobs Adam could almost feel shaking his own body.

What was he supposed to do? What was he supposed to say? A guy who hadn't lived his life underground would know. A guy who wasn't a total freakazoid would know exactly how to comfort her.

He took a tentative step toward Liz, and then she flung herself at him. She wrapped her arms around his shoulders and pressed her face against the front of his T-shirt. He could feel her warm tears soaking through the material to his skin.

"It's okay," he whispered, feeling totally helpless and useless. "Everything is going to be okay."

She shook her head, her face still pressed against him, and her hair tumbled back down. Adam reached out and combed his fingers through it in long, even strokes. "It really is going to be okay," he repeated.

He tried to keep his thoughts away from the fact that Liz's body was touching his. This was so not the time. But his skin turned to fire at every contact point, and Adam could hardly breathe with wanting her. His hands longed to explore the curves of her body, experience the texture of her skin. Adam denied them. He kept lightly brushing Liz's hair.

He remembered having a nightmare when he was a little boy in the compound. One of the guards, a woman, had come into his glass cell and sat on his bed. She'd stroked his hair until he'd fallen back asleep. That was what Liz needed from him right now. Warmth, not heat.

Gradually the sobs shuddering through her body grew gentler, then stopped. Liz lifted her head.

"Sorry," she mumbled without looking at him. She brushed at the wet spot on the front of his T-shirt, the light pressure of her fingers sending jolts through his body. "Sorry I bawled all over you."

He gently pulled her hand away from his shirt. "Don't worry about it." He started to release her, but her fingers twined around his. Adam marveled at how he could feel that touch all the way down to the arches of his feet.

"You're so sweet," Liz said, finally looking at him. They were almost exactly the same height, so her dark brown eyes met his evenly. She leaned closer and kissed him on the corner of his mouth. Adam didn't have a chance to react before it was over, before his first kiss ever was over.

"You're sweet, too," Adam answered, although the word was totally inadequate to describe Liz. His eyes dropped to her lips, her beautifully shaped, beautifully full lips. Michael said it's okay for friends to kiss, he thought.

It was as if the thought propelled him forward. He hesitated with his lips a fraction of an inch away from hers. She didn't pull away, so he kissed her, a kiss only seconds longer than hers had been.

Or at least it would have been that short if Liz hadn't cupped the back of his head with one hand, keeping his mouth on hers. It's like all my molecules are . . . dancing, Adam thought fuzzily.

Then he felt Liz's tongue teasing open his lips, and all thought slammed to a halt. Adam was thrown into a universe of pure sensation—hot, wet, sweet.

Liz.

Adam pulled Liz closer, greedy for even more. She responded by sliding her hands up under his shirt, her palms running across his bare back.

He pushed her thick hair to one side so his fingers could taste the skin at the base of her neck. He felt a little shiver rip through her, and he was awed by the realization that he could have that effect on her. On *Liz*.

Adam wrenched his lips away from her mouth, hating to leave it but needing to continue discovering her, needing to make her shiver again. He traced the line of her jaw with his tongue, then moved down and concentrated on the hollow of her throat, sucking at the tender center, scraping his teeth lightly against her collarbone.

Liz shivered again, then she slowly eased herself away from him. "We can't. . . . We have to stop."

Adam's ability to think slowly returned. "Why?" he asked, his body screaming to return to hers.

"Max," Liz said simply.

The name was like a gallon of ice water thrown over Adam.

"Right. Max," he repeated.

"I used to hang out here a lot, when things got too intense at one of my homes. It's the cave where our pods were left until it was time for us to break free," Michael told Trevor. "There's a sleeping bag over there." He pointed to the back of the cave. "And there are some canteens and food stashed in that hole I carved out of the limestone."

"Thanks," Trevor said. He walked over and sat down on the bag. Michael sat down next to him and leaned back against the hard, cool wall.

What if Trevor *is* dangerous?

The thought flashed through Michael's head so fast, he didn't have time to stop it. He glanced over at Trevor. He hoped his brother hadn't seen any trace of suspicion in Michael's aura.

"Sorry about what happened back at the museum," Michael said. They hadn't talked about it during the drive out to the cave. They'd just listened to the radio and pretended everything was normal.

"I guess I should have said something, defended myself. I was just too blown away," Trevor said. He gave a harsh bark of laugher. "No one's ever called me a killer before."

"You've got to get out more," Michael joked. Or tried to. It sounded funnier in his head. That seemed to happen a lot with Trevor, the sounded-better-in-the-head phenomenon.

"I almost could see the humans being suspicious of me, but . . ." Trevor let his words trail off.

"It's not a nonhuman-human thing," Michael explained. He shifted slightly, trying to find a position where the cave wall wouldn't dig into his spine. "If you'd asked me six months ago, I'd have told you that there was no way a human could be trusted not to murder you in your sleep."

The word *murder* seemed to come out of his mouth louder than the others. What if Max is right about Trevor? Michael thought again.

Michael squeezed his hand into a fist, grinding

the bits of glass deeper, hoping the pain would bring back his righteous anger, his absolute certainty that Max and Alex had no clue what Trevor was really about. It didn't.

"There have been tons of times when Alex, Liz, and Maria have put their own lives in danger to save me, Max, and Isabel," Michael continued, suddenly feeling very tired. He stretched out onto his back. But it felt weird to be lying down with Trevor still sitting up, so Michael shoved himself upright again.

"So I know for sure that nothing that was said tonight had anything to do with who is human and who isn't. Actually, I don't even think Maria necessarily believed that Alex was right about you," Michael rushed on. "And Liz—Liz is totally logical. When she hears about this, I can guarantee you she won't jump to any conclusions."

Although logic might tell Liz to err on the side of caution. Logic might tell her that they should all stay very far away from Trevor if and until they were absolutely sure he wasn't a threat.

"What about Isabel?" Trevor asked, his gray eyes glittering with intensity.

"I think Izzy was withholding judgment," Michael answered. "It looked like she wanted to hear everything before she made up her mind."

"But she's willing to consider the possibility that I would have killed Alex for the Stone if I could," Trevor said, bitterness edging his voice.

123

Michael thought about the cool way Isabel had asked her questions back at the museum. "I'm not going to lie to you—I think Isabel is in guilty-until-proven-innocent mode." He took a deep breath. "Too much has happened to her—to all of us, I guess—to make it that easy to trust people."

"I don't have to ask what Max thought," Trevor said.

Michael reached into the hole in the cave wall, pulled down a battered metal canteen, and took a long swig. "Grape soda and soy sauce. Want some?"

Trevor took the canteen, tilted back his head, and let some of the drink pour down his throat. "Excellent," he said.

"We're pretty much the only ones who think so—not even Max, Izzy, or Adam will drink it," Michael answered.

Trevor and I are so much alike, Michael thought. Why can't Max see that?

"The thing with Max . . ." Michael paused, not sure exactly what he wanted to say. "Max is practically like my brother. It's just that, lately . . ." He shook his head. "I don't know, since he went through his *akino* and joined the consciousness, he's been changing. Sometimes it's like he's not even Max anymore."

"Yeah, that happens a lot," Trevor answered. "A lot of the beings come to the Kindred because they refused to join the consciousness. They didn't want to lose their sense of self. You know, their identity."

"Isn't that basically the same as committing suicide?" Michael asked.

"You mean because you'll die if you go through your *akino* without making the connection?" Trevor asked. He handed the canteen to Michael, and Michael shoved it back in the hole. "That's bull," Trevor continued, his voice rough with anger. "That's what the consciousness wants you to think, but it's complete bull."

"No way," Michael said. "I saw Max during his *akino*. He really almost died." Michael still had nightmares where he was forced to attend Max's funeral again and again.

"Do I look alive to you?" Trevor asked.

"Yeah, but—" Michael stared at Trevor. "Are you saying you've already gone through your *akino*?"

"You got it," Trevor answered.

"Is there any way to break the connection?" Michael demanded. "Can Max?"

"The consciousness is too strong for an individual being to break free," Trevor answered. "And I get the feeling that Max is so far along that he wouldn't want to separate himself from the consciousness even if he could."

"Maybe you're right," Michael reluctantly admitted. He shoved himself to his feet. "I've got to take off. I know it sounds stupid, but I don't want to leave Adam alone too long. Can you think of anything else you might need?"

Trevor shook his head and stood up, too. "I've slept in much worse places, that's for sure."

"I'll come by after school tomorrow with some more supplies, but I don't think you'll have to hole up here more than a few days," Michael said. "I'm going to talk to Max and Alex and the others. I'm sure I'll be able to convince them you're not dangerous or anything."

I don't know how, he added to himself. But I'm going to do it. I've got to.

Trevor looked doubtful, but he didn't say anything.

"So, uh, see you," Michael said as he backed toward the mouth of the cave.

"Want me to heal your hand before you go?" Trevor volunteered. "Or do you want to keep walking around dripping blood?"

"I can do it myself," Michael told him quickly.

If he and Trevor connected, Michael would be open to attack. Trevor could just grab a vein in his head and start squeezing.

But that wouldn't happen—because Trevor isn't a killer, Michael told himself. He strode forward and stretched his hand out to his brother.

"Actually, it would be easier if you did it for me."

# NINE

Liz felt fingers brushing her hair away from her face. I have to tell Adam to stop, she thought. But it felt so good. I'll pretend I'm still asleep, she decided. Just for a few minutes more.

"What are you doing here, Liz?" a voice asked. Not Adam's voice. *Max's* voice.

Liz's eyes snapped open, and she saw Max kneeling on the floor next to her. "What are you doing here?" he repeated.

She sat up, Adam's air mattress squeaking under her. He'd insisted that she take it while he slept on the floor. She glanced across the room. He wasn't there now.

"What are you doing here?" Max asked again.

What was wrong with him? He was like a talking doll that someone had stepped on so many times it could say only one thing. "If you'd called me last night the way you were supposed to, you'd know," Liz snapped.

An expression that was part hurt and part guilt flashed across Max's face. "I was going to, but then the consciousness—"

"The consciousness," Liz cut him off. "Of course, the consciousness."

Max stood up and took a step away from her. "I actually came by because I need to talk to Michael," he said, pulling a painfully obvious subject change.

"Michael and Trevor never made it back last night," Liz told him. She felt a little pang as she realized she'd been so caught up in her own garbage, she'd almost forgotten about them. "I heard about what happened," she added, her voice softening.

"Yeah, so it wasn't just because of the consciousness that I didn't call," Max said, leaping on the excuse in what Liz considered pure weasel fashion. "After Alex came and told me that he thought Trevor could be dangerous, things kind of got out of control."

Liz nodded. "I get that," she said. She stood up. She was tired of talking to Max with him towering over her. "And if last night was a one-time thing, it would be no big deal—even though I really needed you."

"Why? What happened?" he asked. His eyes flicked up and down her. "Whoa. Your aura is really in chaos."

Is it just Max looking at me right now? Or is it all the beings? Liz wondered, a prickling, tickling sensation running from the top of her neck all the way down her spine.

"There was a time when you would have noticed that the first second you saw me," she told Max. She

128

pulled down on the hem of Adam's T-shirt, which she'd been using as a nightgown. Suddenly it felt too short.

"Liz, cut me a break," Max shot back, his voice taking on a steely edge. "There's a guy who could be a killer wandering around loose. And not just a guy—Michael's brother."

"No, that's way too easy. You know that's not what's really going on between us," Liz insisted. She snagged the Star Wars comforter off the air mattress and wrapped it tightly around her waist.

"I'd like to hear what you think *is* going on between us," Max said, his voice faintly patronizing. In another second he's going to be asking me if I'm PMS-ing, Liz thought.

"God, Max, I can't even kiss you anymore without you drifting away to the consciousness," she burst out. "Do you know how disgusting that feels? To be kissing someone and then feel their lips get all loose and dead?"

As opposed to Adam's lips, so eager, so warm. Liz shoved that thought away.

"Disgusting," Max repeated. In a flash he had her face cupped between his hands. His eyes bored into hers, then shifted down to her lips.

He's going to try to kiss me, Liz thought with a spurt of panic.

"Yeah, completely disgusting," Liz answered. She reached out and put her fingers on his lips, gently but firmly. "Because it wasn't *you.*"

Max pulled her hand away and backed up. "Disgusting," he repeated again. "So, what are you really saying? Are you saying you don't want to be with me?"

"I want to be with *you*, Max. But you're not you anymore," Liz cried.

Max's brilliant blue eyes got a blank, shuttered look. "So you're breaking up with me?"

Liz felt that ripping, tearing sensation again, just the way she had last night with her parents.

Is there going to be anything left of me? she thought.

But she couldn't pretend that things were the same between her and Max. She couldn't pretend he was still the one she'd fallen in love with, the one she'd loved heart, and soul, and body.

That Max was gone.

"Are you breaking up with me?" Max repeated, voice dead.

How could he expect her to speak? How with this gaping, raw wound inside her?

Liz nodded. And Max turned and walked away.


"So you broke up with Max?" Adam asked. It had taken him all the way through one-and-a-half daytime talk shows to get up the guts to say it.

"Yeah," Liz answered. It wasn't a happy yeah, a now-I'm-free-to-spend-all-day-making-out-with-you-Adam yeah. It was just kind of tired and sad.

130

Adam was worried about her. Her eyes were all puffy, her lips turned down a tiny bit at the corners, and her aura hadn't cleared up any.

"Is that why you decided not to go to school? Too hard to be around him right now?" Adam hated the thought that Liz could care so much about Max, even in a twisted, negative way.

But basically, that was what drew him to Liz. She was so intense about everything. He wanted to make up for every moment he'd lost in the compound, and Liz was a person who did things full out.

"No. Well, I guess it's a side benefit," Liz answered. "I was afraid my father would show up at school, and I don't want to see him." Her aura's deep purple web darkened until it was almost black.

He wanted to do something to make her feel better. But what? Almost as soon as he asked himself the question, an idea popped into his head.

Adam turned his attention to a large section of the floor almost in the middle of the living room. There was no furniture in it. He and Michael were supposed to get some eventually.

"Do you like to trampoline?" he asked Liz.

"Huh?" She looked over at him with a distracted expression.

"Never mind. Just wait," Adam said, smiling to himself. He concentrated on the molecules of wood in the section of the floor and used his power to *push* them farther apart. "Okay, now watch." Adam stood up and walked over to the section of floor he'd modified. His feet sank into it up to his ankles. He shot a look at Liz, then he started to bounce, going so high, his head brushed against the ceiling. Maybe I should temporarily make us a hole up there so we can go even higher, he thought.

But when he looked at Liz again, he knew that wouldn't be necessary. She had this very polite smile on her face. All he'd done was give her the extra burden of trying not to hurt his feelings.

The mole boy again proves that he has failed to grasp the basics of normal social interaction, Adam thought.

He *pushed* the molecules of the floor back into place, then went over and sat down next to Liz. Not too close. He knew enough to know that touching wouldn't be welcome right now.

"I wish I knew what you were feeling," Adam said. "I never had a fight with my dad. I mean, I never had a dad, just Sheriff Valenti. So it's not like I can give you some great advice."

"That's okay," Liz answered. She started twisting her hair into a knot. He'd noticed that she did that almost every time she felt uncomfortable.

"I never told anyone this, but after I killed the Sheriff—" Adam began.

"You didn't kill him," Liz interrupted. "You can't think that way. Elsevan DuPris had control over you."

"Yeah, well, after *my body* killed the sheriff and I found out what I—it—had done, I totally broke down crying the first time I was alone," he admitted.

He glanced at Liz. She had her serious, intent look going. He wasn't sure if this was helping her or not, but it was the only father experience he could share with her.

"I should have hated him, right?" Adam asked. "And I did hate him, too—when I found out the truth. When I found out that there was a whole world he'd locked me away from while he had me do his little experiments. But . . ." Adam paused, not sure how to explain the rest, even to himself.

"But what?" Liz prompted.

"But he used to read me storybooks. And he . . . he was nice to me. And as far as I knew, he was my dad. I felt like I belonged to him. Even when I found out how evil he really was, I guess I didn't want him dead. It's almost like he was part of me, you know? So how could I want him dead?" Adam answered. "Maybe locked away in the compound himself, but not dead."

"I never thought about the sheriff dying as you losing a father," Liz said. "But of course it felt that way to you."

She reached over and took his hand. "Do you have these times where you totally forget he's dead? When my sister died, there would be days where I'd get halfway home from school before I'd remember, especially right after it happened. Like I'd have a story I was planning to tell her, and then—bam!" She made a little explosion with her hands. "It would hit me."

"That's happened to me, too." Adam felt a loosening in his chest. He hadn't realized that he'd really been needing to talk to someone about this. "So when does it stop?"

Liz shrugged. "When it happens, I'll let you know," she answered. Then she turned her head and met his gaze. "It doesn't happen nearly as much anymore. And the realizations are more like, I don't know, like oh-rights than bams."

"I thought everyone would just think I was being a moron if I actually said I felt sad about Valenti," Adam confessed.

"Of course you were sad. He was your papa," Liz reassured him.

But he wondered if she'd switched over to talking more about herself and her own father. If Adam could feel so much for Valenti, how much more must Liz feel for Mr. Ortecho?

"You should talk to him. Your papa," Adam said. He wasn't sure she'd want him butting in, but he thought she needed to hear it.

"You don't get it," Liz burst out. "He pretty much proved he doesn't even know me. He probably thinks he loves me and everything, but how can you love what you don't know?"

"So you're just going to run away?" he demanded. "That's not you, Liz. You fight for things. You want him to know you—make it happen."

"Make it happen," Liz repeated. She snorted.

"Yeah, make it happen," Adam insisted. "You helped break Michael out of the Clean Slate compound. You faked out Elsevan DuPris's bounty hunters. You practically even brought Max back from the dead, the way he tells it. You make things happen all the time. Impossible things."

Liz didn't say anything. She took her hand away and pulled her hair free from its knot, then immediately started twisting her hair back up again.

"You know what's going to happen if you don't, right?" Adam asked. He knew what he was about to say would probably hurt her, but he had to do it, anyway.

Liz shook her head.

"If you don't, someday you're going to be coming home from school—or the job you get after college, or whatever—and you'll be all excited about telling your father some great thing that happened to you. Or even some awful thing," Adam explained. "And then—bam!—it will hit you. You don't talk to your papa anymore."

Max's eyes went right to the group's usual table as soon as he entered the cafeteria. He felt a little of the tension flow out of his body when he spotted Michael sitting there. He hurried over.

"You're alive," he said.

Michael shot him an angry look, and Max belatedly realized this wasn't exactly the time for humor, not that it had exactly *been* humor.

"I stopped by your place this morning, but you weren't there," he continued. "We need to talk." He saw Isabel and Alex heading toward them. Maria would probably show up any second. "Alone, okay?"

"Whatever." Michael didn't sound too happy about it, but he shoved himself up from the table and followed Max to the bio lab. Max knew nobody would be hanging around in there at lunch. At least since Liz wasn't at school today.

He clamped down hard on the pain that shot through him when he thought about her. He couldn't deal with the Liz thing and the Michael thing at the same time. Even separately felt almost impossible.

"You wanted to talk, so talk," Michael said, leaning against one of the lab station counters.

"I wondered what you were able to find out from Trevor last night," Max told him.

"I wasn't trying to find out anything," Michael shot back. He picked up one of the Bunsen burner strikers and flicked it, producing a few sparks. "I wasn't with him to do some kind of undercover work for you."

"I didn't mean it that way." Max slumped down on one of the tall stools across from Michael.

"Look, according to the consciousness, Trevor could be a threat to all of us. You should have felt the fury coming off the beings when I sent out an image of him."

Max saw Michael stiffen, and he rushed on before Michael could interrupt him. "I didn't get any sense that Trevor is a killer, but that's what Alex felt from him in the wormhole. I just want to know if there's anything you and Trevor talked about that will help me get all this straight."

Michael flicked the striker a few more times, then tossed it behind him. "Have you ever considered the possibility that the consciousness could be lying to you?"

It was as if Michael had sucker punched him. Max actually felt a little dizzy, a little wobbly perched on the stool. He stuck one foot down to steady himself.

Max had linked himself to the consciousness for life. He was a part of it. It was a part of him. If it could lie . . . if it could have some kind of *evil* intent . . .

No. Impossible. His parents were part of the consciousness. Ray was part of the consciousness.

"The consciousness isn't a single entity," Max explained, talking to himself as much as Michael. "It's an immense collection of beings—the number of them is practically unfathomable. I don't get how something of that size and structure could lie."

"Well, how do you explain the fact that Trevor

went through his *akino* and lived?" Michael asked. "I mean, according to the consciousness, you don't join, you die."

Wait, did that mean Max hadn't had to join? Did that mean—

Max shook his head. He realized there was a very obvious answer to Michael's question. But it didn't seem that Michael had given it a thought.

"Have you ever considered the possibility that *Trevor* could be lying to *you?*" Max asked, trying very hard to keep his tone nonconfrontational.

"He's my brother," Michael answered, as if that said it all.

Max stood up so fast, he knocked the stool over. "So am I," he insisted. "In every way that matters, I'm your brother, too."

Didn't Michael get it? Didn't he understand that the bond between them was deeper than the one created by being born of the same parents? He and Michael had shared every important experience of their lives. Michael and Trevor were practically strangers.

"If that's true, if you're my brother, then why don't you trust me?" Michael exploded. He shoved himself away from the counter. "I'm out of here."

Max watched him leave. He wanted to call Michael back, but what was the point? Michael had made his choice.

Max stood up and turned on the faucet next to

him. He stuck his face under and let the water pour over him until his skin turned numb with cold. Then he snapped off the faucet and dried himself off with one of the rough brown paper towels.

Then he heard a little squeaking behind him.

"You're not going to give me grief, too, are you, Fred?" he asked. He walked over to the cage of white mice and pulled out the skinniest one. He stared into its little red eyes. "Remember, you owe me. I saved your life once. I saved Michael and Liz's lives too, not that they're bothering to be grateful."

Fred squeaked again. Max pretended he could understand him. "Yeah, I know." Max sighed. "They've saved my life at least once each. So I should go try and work things out with them before someone wanders by and sees me going all Doctor Doolittle."

He put Fred back in the cage, then felt a tingle of curiosity from the consciousness. No. No way. There are some things I won't do, he thought.

The tingle grew to an insistent electric sizzle.

"Okay, fine," Max muttered. He picked up one of the food pellets from the mice's dish and popped it into his mouth.

The blend of flavors was more complex than he'd expected. He closed his eyes and chewed slowly, sharing the experience with the other beings.

# TEN

Liz pulled out her key and then stood there on the porch, staring at her front door. Adam is right, she told herself. You have to do this. You have to at least try.

She slid her key into the lock, but before she could turn it, the door flew open and she was in her mother's arms.

"*Mija*, we were so worried. Where were you?" She pulled away and gave Liz's shoulders a little shake, then hugged her again.

"I stayed with friends," Liz said when her mama finally let her go. "I couldn't be in the same house with Papa. I just couldn't."

Her mother was wearing the same overalls she'd had on last night. She looked as if she hadn't slept at all. "Liz, your father loves you more than life. You know that, don't you?"

"He doesn't even know me. I know that you don't think I'm like . . . I shouldn't have said that to you. But Papa does," Liz said softly. "He thinks I'm this person who needs to be under a twenty-four/seven drug overdose prevention watch." Liz felt tears sting her eyes, and she blinked them away.

"He just wants you to be safe," her mother answered. She turned Liz around and gave her a gentle push down the hall. "He's in the backyard. Go talk to him."

Liz hesitated. Isn't this what you came here for? she asked herself. Then she strode directly to the big glass door, slid it open, and stepped outside. Her father was lying on the grass with his eyes shut.

Automatically she listened for the music that would give her a clue to how her papa was feeling. But the backyard was silent. It was so weird. Her father even had one of those waterproof radios. He couldn't stand to be without his tunes long enough to take a shower.

Liz took a step forward, then glanced back toward the house. Maybe she should go get her mother. Maybe it would be better to do this as a three-way talk. Maybe—

"Did she call yet?" Liz's papa asked, without opening his eyes.

"Aren't you cold?" Liz said. He wasn't even wearing a jacket.

Her father sat up slowly and shoved himself around to face her. She waited for him to start yelling or to at least say something, but he didn't. What was he thinking? Was he waiting for her to apologize, or—

Just say what you've got to say, she told herself.

142

"I have a question," she announced. "Do you think it's possible for someone to be—at least very likely be—valedictorian while getting high on a regular basis?" she asked. "Do you think someone doing tons of drugs would remember to call *every time* she wasn't going to come home straight after school? Or—"

Liz had almost half a lifetime of examples, but her throat had gotten too tight for any more words of her logical argument to squeak through. I'm going to cry, she thought, horrified. She never cried in front of her parents. Never. It was part of being the daughter who made up for the daughter who died.

And suddenly she was sobbing, sobbing as hard as she had in the museum. But now no one's arms were around her. Now she was standing all alone, with her father miles and miles away, just looking at her.

"I tried . . . everything perfect," she choked out. "Grades . . . at the Crashdown . . . room clean. God, everything." Liz swiped her arm across her eyes, but the tears kept coming. She rushed on. "Can't do anything to make Mama and Papa worry. Can't do anything that might scare them . . . and make them think that I . . . that I was going to turn out like Rosa. Have to be perfect, perfect, perfect."

"Well, you're not perfect," her father said. He pushed himself to his feet with a little grunt but didn't move toward her. "You always hog all your *abuela's* green sauce."

A surprised laugh escaped Liz. She wiped away her tears again, and this time they stayed gone.

Her papa smiled at her. "See, I know you. Rosa liked red sauce, Liz likes green sauce. Rosa liked to color, and Liz played Roller Derby in the driveway. Rosa always said, 'Papa, tell me a story.' And Liz always said, 'Papa, I have a question.'" He shook his head. "You used to ask me the most amazing things. 'Papa, I have a question—do butterflies remember that they used to be caterpillars, or do they look at caterpillars and just think, eww, gross?'"

"I don't remember that," Liz admitted.

"I do. I remember everything about you," her father answered. He walked over and took her hand, the way he used to when she was a little girl. It almost made Liz start to cry again.

"I know you're not Rosa," he said, meeting her gaze squarely and directly. "You have never given me any reason to think that you were getting yourself into the kind of danger she was." He squeezed her hand. "But I didn't see it in Rosa. I was her papa, and I didn't see it. I have to live with that. But I don't . . . I can't . . ."

"I know, I know," Liz answered. She squeezed his hand back. "You won't have to. I promise."

They started toward the house, then Liz's father paused and pointed up to the flying pig weather vane on the top of their house. "Remember how Rosa used to say that I bought that just so she'd be too embarrassed to have any of her friends come over?"

Liz smiled. It was like now that he'd finally started talking about Rosa, he couldn't stop.

"Yeah, she even had a name for it. What was it?" Liz asked.

"It kept changing. Mr. Sausagestuff was one of the less raunchy ones," he answered. He led her to the sliding door, and he didn't drop her hand when they stepped inside.

"Papa, I have a question," Liz said. Then she stopped herself. In the last few minutes they'd talked more about Rosa than they had since she died. But maybe her question would be pushing things too far.

"What? Ask it," her father urged, sensing her hesitation.

"I was wondering what happened to all the pictures of Rosa," Liz said. "There's not even one in the whole house, and I—I miss them."

Her father's grip on her hand tightened painfully. Liz shot a worried glance at his face. There were tears in his eyes. Liz didn't think she'd ever seen her papa even this close to crying.

"It's not important," Liz said quickly. She'd hurt him, maybe more than he could bear. Why did she—

"Estela," her papa called out.

Liz's mama appeared in the doorway an instant later. She's been going nuts this whole time, I bet, Liz thought.

"Liz and I wanted to look at some pictures of

Rosa. Do you know where they are?" he asked.

"I—yes, I'll go get them." Liz's mother smiled at them, a quavering smile, but a smile. "I'd like to look at them, too."

"Are you carless?" Maria heard Michael call as she headed out of the school.

"Yes, unfortunately, I'm almost always sans car," she answered when he caught up to her.

"I could give you a ride," he offered as he slung his backpack over one shoulder.

"Oooh, a ride in that big car of yours. That's so sweet." Maria batted her eyes at him, almost tripping over the curb as they started across the parking lot. "I hear that you own your own apartment and a business, too. Is that true?" She ran her fingers up and down his arm in an exaggerated flirt maneuver.

Hey, if she could touch him and stay in buddy mode by pretending she was just goofing around, why not? Well, except for the fact that it left her feeling like a dog that had been teased by a piece of meat hanging just out of reach over its head.

"That's right, sweetcakes. Now all I need is a little arm trophy, and I'm set. I could probably get you an . . . audition, if you're interested in the position," Michael answered.

But she could tell his heart wasn't in it. The boy was troubled. As soon as they were both settled in his car, she turned to him and said, "Okay, come on. Tell Dr. Maria everything."

"What?" Michael asked, looking at her like she was nuts.

"What?" she repeated, looking at him like he was nuts, mocking him.

Michael started the car and got in the line of vehicles moving out onto the street. He kept his eyes locked on the windshield.

"Oh, you want me to use my famous psychic powers." Maria wiggled her fingers at him. "I see Max. I see Trevor. I see you in the middle," she intoned, trying to do some kind of Romanian gypsy accent.

"Max is practically forcing me to take sides against him," Michael burst out. "He won't even consider the possibility that the consciousness could be wrong about Trevor."

"Max doesn't like to take chances with the safety of the group," Maria reminded him. "You know him—Mr. Responsibility."

Michael got his turn at the driveway and pulled out onto the street. "What he doesn't seem to get is that Trevor is my brother," he answered. "My brother isn't going to be a threat to the group."

"You don't know that for sure," Maria said as gently as she could. She felt so awful for Michael. He'd been wanting a real family his whole life. He should be in the midst of a party marathon, showing

Trevor everything, doing brother stuff. But instead Michael's best friend—let's be real, practically Michael's *other* brother—was trying to convince Michael that his only living family member was a deranged killer.

"So you agree with Max?" Michael demanded. He screeched the car to a stop at a red light.

Maria shot out her hands and braced herself on the dashboard. "I'm thinking you might be more dangerous," she muttered. But at the hurt that she could see in Michael's gray eyes—the hurt he was working so hard to hide—she relented.

"I'm not sure what to think," she admitted. She couldn't tell him that she was positive, absolutely positive, that Trevor was a wonderful guy—even though she knew that's what Michael wanted to hear. "Alex and Max both seem pretty sure that there's some kind of—of *problem*. I just want us all to be careful until we figure out exactly what it is."

"But you'll at least give him a chance?" Michael asked as he turned onto her street. "That's all I ask, that you don't make any assumptions about him until you get to know him."

"I will absolutely, totally give him a chance," Maria promised. She had to do that much for Michael, even though her intuition was twanging away inside her, telling her it was a bad, bad idea.

Neither Alex nor Max was the type to jump to conclusions. If they both thought Trevor could be dangerous, they were probably right.

Michael swung into her driveway and stopped the car—a nice, gentle stop this time.

"You want to come in?" Maria asked. "I promised Kevin I'd help him do a mock newspaper for social studies. You should hear his headlines about Magellan. He makes the guy sound like a comic book hero."

"Sure, why not?" Michael answered. "Although I was hoping I could talk you into making brownies or something for Trevor. I'm meeting up with him later."

"We'll do that, too," Maria said. She hopped out of the car, happy to have something nice to do for Michael's brother that wasn't potentially life threatening. "Should I do my carob ones or the—"

"The other ones, definitely," Michael said as he followed her into the house. "Maybe with white vinegar icing."

Maria made a gagging sound. "It will keep Kevin from snagging any, at least," she answered. "Kevin, the clock's ticking," she shouted. "I told you, I'm not staying up until two A.M. like last time."

"Maybe we beat him home," Michael suggested.

"He should have been here at least half an hour ago. But it doesn't look like he came in and then went out again. It's way too neat." Kevin usually started tossing things the second he hit the hall—backpack here, coat there, shoes on the coffee table. "I guess I should check the fridge for a note, just in case he grew a completely new personality and left one."

She hurried into the kitchen, Michael right behind her. She spotted a bright orange sheet of paper under one of the magnets. "Color me amazed," she said. She dropped her backpack on one of the kitchen chairs and grabbed the note.

She sank down on the kitchen floor as she read it. She didn't even think about the chair a few feet away from her.

"What?" Michael demanded.

The note fluttered like a hummingbird's wing as she handed it to him. She couldn't make her fingers stop shaking even when she knotted her hands together.

Michael read it out loud. "You give me what I want. I give you what you want." He sat down on the floor next to Maria. "I don't get it."

Maria swallowed hard. "It's not from Kevin. I think it's from . . ." She stared down at her hands, not even able to look at Michael. How could she look at him when she was thinking what she was thinking? But what she was thinking was the only thing that made any sense.

"Michael, I think the note's from Trevor," she finally said.

"What are you talking about?" Michael flipped the note over, then flipped it back. "I don't see anything that—"

"Kevin?" Maria yelled sharply. "Kevin!" The house was empty. "Don't you get it?" Maria cried, what little self-control she had snapping. "It's a ransom note! Don't you get it? Trevor kidnapped Kevin. He's not going to give Kevin back until we hand over the Stone!"

"I think Michael's right. We shouldn't necessarily trust the consciousness, at least not blindly," Liz declared from the backseat of his car.

Thank God for Liz, Michael thought. And Adam. At least they were adding some sanity to the group. And Isabel was still doing her Switzerland impersonation—totally neutral so far. But Max, Maria, and Alex were in full-throttle Trevor-is-evil-incarnate mode.

"Can't you go any faster?" Maria cried, clearly a breath away from all-out hysteria.

Michael pressed the accelerator down a little harder. "This car isn't exactly designed for desert driving," he told her. "But we're almost to the cave."

"Kevin is going to be fine," Max said from the shotgun seat.

"Yeah," Alex agreed. "Trevor's smart enough to know that he has to keep Kevin safe or he won't have any value as a bargaining chip."

Maria let out a little moan. Alex winced. "Sorry," he told her. "I was trying to be encouraging. I forgot to give you the nonstupid translation."

"We should have taken the Jeep, too. I hate getting all squished," Isabel complained. Then she looked over her shoulder at Maria. "Sorry. I forgot to give you the non-self-centered translation."

"It's better that we only took one car," Michael said. "I don't think it's a good idea to convoy to the cave. It could get noticed."

It wasn't the real reason he'd wanted them all in one car. He didn't want anyone getting to Trevor without him. The only reason he'd even told them Trevor's whereabouts was so that Trevor could prove he was innocent.

"I don't know why you say that we shouldn't trust the consciousness," Max said to Liz, although he said it without turning around to look at her. "I mean, just because it interferes with us kissing—"

"That's not why," Liz snapped. "Have you forgotten what the consciousness did to you, Max? It used you as a killing machine. Don't try to pretend you weren't sickened when it made you attack DuPris because I know you were."

"The consciousness also almost killed you," Isabel added. "It sucked out so much of your strength to open the wormhole that you almost died."

Is she coming around to my side? Michael wondered.

"That was necessary," Max insisted.

"Besides, it's not just information from the consciousness we're going on, remember?" Alex asked. "I felt—"

"We're here," Michael interrupted.

He jumped out of the car and sprinted to the crack in the desert that opened into the cave. He wanted to give Trevor a few seconds warning before he was descended upon.

"You've got company," he called. *"Lots of company."* He swung himself down onto the big rock and jumped onto the cave floor from there.

He did a quick check of the cave. Trevor was alone.

Of course he is, Michael thought. You knew he would be. But Michael still felt relieved.

"I wasn't expecting you this early," Trevor said. He stood up from Michael's sleeping bag and headed toward him.

"Look, we think someone kidnapped Maria's brother and—" Michael began, speaking as rapidly as he could.

Before he could get out the explanation, Maria half leaped, half fell into the cave.

"Where's Kevin?" she shouted. She lunged at Trevor, but Michael caught her before she could reach him. He wrapped one arm across her shoulders and held her against him.

"We're going to find out everything," Michael told her. "We're going to get Kevin back, I promise."

The tension in Maria's body didn't ease at all. Michael wished there was something he could say to her, something to *make* her believe. But he didn't think she trusted him enough right now to have faith in him. The thought was like a boulder in Michael's chest.

Max scrambled into the cave, with Alex right behind him.

"See? No Kevin," Michael announced.

"Just because he's not here doesn't mean Trevor didn't take him," Max shot back.

"It doesn't mean he *did*, either," Liz said as she hopped down onto the rock and then moved over so Isabel could climb down.

Trevor turned to Michael. "Would you please tell me what the hell is going on?"

"I'll tell you what the hell is going on," Maria cried. She wrenched herself away from Michael and went toe to toe with Trevor. "You kidnapped my brother so we'd give you the Stone. Now where is he?"

Trevor shook his head and stared up at the roof of the cave. "Unbelievable. First I was a killer, and now I'm a kidnapper."

At least Trevor's trying to stay cool, Michael thought. He gave his brother a nod of encouragement.

"Why don't you come back tomorrow?" Trevor smiled at Maria, or at least he twisted his lips in an attempt at a smile. It came out more like a grimace. "By then I'll probably only be a bank robber or something."

"You *knew* Kevin was important to the group!" Maria yelled. She lurched forward and pounded on Trevor's chest with both fists. He didn't even try to defend himself. "That's why you asked all those questions about him at the party!"

Michael hauled Maria away from Trevor again. She fought violently in his arms.

"That's why you took him!" she screamed at Trevor. "Because you know we all care about him, and because he's small and weak and can't defend himself."

"Shhh, Maria," Michael murmured in her ear. "Shhh. Kevin is okay. He's okay."

Maria twisted around to face him, her face so twisted with fear and fury that it was almost unrecognizable. "You don't know that!" she screamed. "You're just refusing to accept that you're wrong about Trevor. And Kevin could be out there somewhere dying! Don't you even care?"

Alex rushed up to them. He put his hand on Maria's shoulder, and she flung herself at him. She wrapped her arms around his neck, ragged sobs making her body heave.

The weight in Michael's chest doubled in size as he watched Liz and Isabel join Alex, surrounding Maria in a protective circle. A circle that kept Michael on the outside. He turned a helpless look on Trevor.

Trevor gave a low growl of frustration. "If I was the kidnapper, right now I'd be telling you that I'd give you a map to your brother's location as soon as you handed over the Stone," he said impatiently.

"But I'm not doing that. Why?" He glanced from person to person.

"Because you're not the kidnapper," Adam finally said from his spot under the cave's entrance.

"Are the rest of you listening?" Michael demanded.

"What Trevor said makes some sense," Liz said, her arm still locked around Maria's waist.

"It's also what an intelligent kidnapper would say right now," Alex protested. He stared at Trevor over the top of Maria's head, his eyes narrow. "And no one is doubting Trevor's intelligence."

"And there's no one else who has a reason to take Kevin," Max added.

"Don't you have any real enemies?" Trevor asked.

"There's DuPris," Michael answered quickly. "DuPris would love to have another one of the Stones." He shot Max and Alex challenging looks, daring them to deny the truth.

"How would DuPris have gotten *behind* me in the wormhole?" Alex asked.

Michael shoved his hands into his pockets, fighting the urge to slam his fist into the cave wall. Alex was right. DuPris couldn't have been in the wormhole. "Who else?" he muttered. "There has to be somebody else."

"There is," Isabel said suddenly. Everyone turned to look at her. Her eyes hardened as she spoke. "Kyle Valenti."

# ELEVEN

"Michael, Liz, Trevor, Adam—you circle around back in case Kyle tries to bolt," Max instructed. "The rest of us will go straight to the front door."

He was almost surprised when the group split into the teams he'd specified with no argument. At least we finally found something we can agree on, he thought as Michael's team headed out.

For now. Max still had a bad feeling about Michael's brother. But it wouldn't hurt to check out the Kyle situation. He was praying that Kyle did have Kevin. If not, Max didn't know what was going to go down between him and Michael. And of course, Trevor himself.

He dug the heel of his hand into his forehead and twisted it back and forth, trying to get some relief from the headache that had kicked in during the drive to the cave.

"Max, let's go," Maria urged. "The others should be around back by now."

"Okay, let's do it." He led the way up to Kyle's front door and knocked. The door swung open immediately. Kyle smirked at them, appearing obscenely self-satisfied.

"Where is he, Valenti?" Max demanded.

"Kevin?" Maria shouted, trying to peer around Kyle. "Are you in there?"

"I'm glad you decided to tell me what I want to know," Kyle said.

Max charged forward, knocking Kyle back into the house. He slammed him against the wall of the front hall and jammed his forearm across Kyle's throat. "No, you're telling *us* what we want to know. Where's Kevin?"

He raised his fist and aimed it at Kyle's face. He was going to have to do this the old-fashioned way. It wasn't safe to use his power. "Talk," he ordered.

Before Kyle could say anything, Max heard the rest of the group burst into the back of the house. "You got him?" Michael shouted.

"Got him," Max called back. Not using my power isn't going to be any kind of problem, he thought. He could feel Alex crowding him, and a second later Michael, Trevor, Adam, and Liz burst into the hall, the fury coming off them like heat waves.

No, dividing Kyle into small enough pieces so everyone could get a shot at him—that was the problem. But Kyle, for some reason, didn't look worried.

"I'm not asking you again," Max warned him.

"You hit me, you never get Kevin back," Kyle said calmly.

Stalemate.

Max glanced at Michael. It was automatic. No matter what had been going on between them lately, when Max thought of backup, he thought of Michael.

"Oh, I'm sure that we could come up with something painful enough—*long* and painful enough—to get you squealing," Michael answered.

Kyle raised one eyebrow. "Possibly," he answered. He pinned Maria with his gaze. "But are you willing to risk it? He's your brother."

"Don't let him mess with you," Alex told her.

"Kevin!" Maria shrieked again. "Are you in here?"

Max heard a sound. Very faint. Possibly nothing. But possibly—

Max jerked Kyle away from the wall and pushed him toward Alex. "Keep him here," he ordered.

"My pleasure," Alex answered. A second later Kyle was on the ground and Alex was kneeling on his chest.

Max started down the hall. He heard footsteps behind him. He glanced back. Michael and Trevor.

The thought of Trevor covering his back wasn't a happy one, but there was no time to battle it out. Max jerked open the first door on the left. Obviously Kyle's bedroom. Total sty. No Kevin.

Michael pushed past him and strode to the closet. He flung open the door. No Kevin.

Max rushed to the next room—Sheriff Valenti's office. Papers strewn everywhere. No Kevin.

"Kevin, if you can hear us, try to make a sound," Trevor shouted.

Where did the guy get off? He'd been on earth for like a day and he was—

Not now, Max told himself. He listened hard and thought he heard a muffled thumping. "What do you think? Under the—"

"Yeah," Michael answered. "Under the floor. There must be a crawl space."

He took the lead, Max and Trevor right behind him. As they entered the master bedroom Max felt a tingle from the consciousness. Some of the beings were interested in the texture of the bedspread.

Automatically he took a step toward the bed. Then he jerked himself away and turned down the volume on the consciousness as low as it could go. He could still feel the beings urging him to go over and run his hands across the material, maybe climb on it and roll around. But it was at a level he could ignore.

"Got it," Michael announced. He yanked open a small, square trapdoor.

"I'm going in," Max said. He strode over and lowered himself through the opening. "Stay here. I'll hand him up to you," he told Michael.

He crouched down until his head was low enough to clear the ceiling of the crawl space. The

160

darkness under the house was no problem for Max. He spotted Kevin almost instantly.

"Your sister's upstairs," he called as he crawled on his hands and knees toward the boy. Kevin gave a muffled cry through his gag. It looked like Kyle had stuffed a tennis ball in Kevin's mouth and then duct taped it into place. A rush of pure hatred overtook Max. Kyle's lucky Kevin didn't suffocate, Max thought. He is so very lucky.

"Almost there, almost there," he told Kevin. Max felt a nail in one of the beams rip through his shirt and slice down his back. He ignored it. "Okay, got you." He reached out and ripped the duct tape off Kevin's mouth with one quick pull.

Kevin clawed the tennis ball out of his mouth and took a long, gasping breath. "Why?" he choked out.

Max hadn't been expecting that question. "The guy's one sick little puppy," he answered, hoping Kevin wouldn't push the issue.

"Let's get out of here. Think you can crawl all right?"

Kevin gave him a *duh* look. "If you untie my hands and feet," he answered.

Max quickly untied the clothesline that bound Kevin. Maybe I should keep this, he thought. Give Kyle a little taste of what he did to this kid.

The second he was free, Kevin was crawling toward the square of light in the open trapdoor. He was faster than Max. Sometimes it helps to be small, Max thought as the same nail got him a second time.

"It smells like mouse poop down here," Kevin complained. He squirmed his way over to the trapdoor.

Max smiled. If Kevin was feeling good enough to whine, he was fine.

"Yeah, it does," Max agreed. "We're coming up," he called to Michael. But Kevin was already hauling himself into the closet.

A moment later a hand reached down to Max. He grabbed it and used it to pull himself up. Two realizations hit him as his head cleared the trapdoor.

It was Trevor helping him out.

And Trevor had his free hand in Max's pocket.

The volume on his connection with the consciousness went all the way up. A shriek of warning ripped through Max, so strong, a shower of red dots streaked past his eyes.

"Michael, he's going for the Stone!" Max shouted.

Michael jerked his attention away from Kevin. Trevor had Max pinned half in and half out of the crawl space. Max had both his hands locked around one of Trevor's wrists. Michael could see Max's arms trembling with the effort to keep Trevor's hand from reaching back into his pocket.

"What the hell are you doing?" he shouted at his brother.

"What's necessary," Trevor yelled back, without turning toward Michael.

Power began to build up in the room. Michael could feel it vibrating through the floor, through the walls, through his body. He didn't know who was getting charged up, Max or Trevor or both, but he knew that the amount of power he was feeling could do some serious damage.

The power let go, and Trevor flew across the room. He slammed into the dresser, shattering the big mirror above it.

Michael bolted toward him, but Trevor was on his feet instantly. His eyes were cool and determined as he advanced on Max.

"Why aren't you doing something?" Kevin shouted.

Because I don't know what to do, Michael felt like shouting back. Any course of action meant hurting Max or his brother. Michael's eyes flicked back and forth between them. Max was standing by the closet, still, but *ready.*

Trevor paced back and forth, studying Max. Then he gave a growl of fury and leaped at him. He was clearly using his power to propel himself because he was flying at Max bullet-fast.

"Trevor, pull back," Michael screamed. If he hit Max at that velocity—

But before Trevor could touch Max, there was another power detonation. Trevor somersaulted through the air. He crashed into the ceiling, then fell to the floor with enough force to send a shudder through the house.

"Do you need me?" Adam cried from down the hall.

"No," Michael shouted back. "Stay where you are." Anyone in this room had a very good chance of getting hurt.

He hoped Trevor would just stay down, but a moment later he was on his feet, clearly having turned his healing powers on himself.

"Give it up, Trevor, you're no match for me. Not when I still have this." Max reached into his pocket and pulled out the Stone. It was glowing more brightly than it ever had, throwing its blue-green light onto Max's face, making him look like a stranger.

"Trevor, he's right," Michael said quickly. "The Stone has more power than you can imagine. This is over."

"It's not over until I'm dead," Trevor announced.

"Your choice," Max answered.

Michael had to diffuse this situation. Now. He turned to Max.

"You don't need to kill him. You have all the control here," he said, going for the logical approach. "Just use the Stone to immobilize him, then we'll figure out what to do."

"Thanks for the support, brother," Trevor said.

"You lied to me," Michael shot back, without

taking his eyes off Max. "You lost the right to my support."

But that didn't mean he was going to let his brother die.

The glow on Max's face intensified as the Stone shone brighter and brighter. "What's it going to be, Trevor?" he demanded.

"Max, get a grip," Michael cried. But Max's face was blank. He was so deeply connected to the consciousness, it was like he wasn't even in the room anymore. Michael could reason with Max, but he knew he had no influence over this Max *thing*.

Michael's heart felt like it was about to hurl itself out of his chest. "Trevor, you've got to walk away," he said, turning all his attention to his brother. "You go after him, it's suicide."

"I have no problem with that," he answered.

The glow of the Stone had become so bright, it was making Michael's eyes water. He shot a quick glance over at Max. Max had the hand holding the Stone stretched out in front of him now. Aimed at Trevor.

Michael didn't think. He just reacted to the threat. He lowered his shoulder and went at Max low and fast.

Max never saw it coming. He went down as easily as a bowling pin. Michael knocked the Stone out of his hand, and it rolled across the floor.

"You've got to snap out of it," Michael yelled. He

grabbed Max and shook him hard. He thought he saw a little awareness come back into his friend's eyes. Michael shook him again.

"Get out of the way, Michael," Trevor said, his voice like ice.

Michael twisted around and stared at his brother. Trevor had the Stone now. It's blue-green light was too brilliant to look at directly. And it was aimed at Max.

"No," Michael said. He positioned himself between Max and Trevor. "No."

"What is going—," Max began, sounding groggy.

"Just stay down," Michael barked.

"Max is a vessel of the consciousness, and he must die," Trevor answered. "Move out of the way."

"No," Michael repeated again. He could hardly see Trevor through the glare from the Stone.

"Michael, the consciousness is evil. If I could pull Max away from it, I would. But it's not possible," Trevor answered. "Now move." His voice was ragged with emotion now, not icy as it had been.

"No." Michael didn't move. He wasn't going to move.

"Guys, Kyle's coming your way," Alex shouted from the front of the house. "He tried to pull a Tyson on me and got loose."

Michael didn't even spare a glance at the door, even when he heard it fly open. Kyle was the least of their problems now.

"Don't make me kill you," Trevor begged.

"I'm not making you kill me," Michael told him. "Just put down—"

Suddenly a piercing metallic screech filled the room, the sound so high, Michael thought it was going to burst his eardrums.

Then the world went white. The floor bucked, and Michael was in the air. Flying through the white. The blazing white light.

It felt like it took him an eternity to hit the ground. When he could breathe again, he struggled to his knees and groped the floor in front of him. He had to find Max, but all he could see was a swirl of white dots in front of his eyes.

Trevor had used the power of the Stone.

"Max!" Michael shouted. "Are you okay?"

Michael blinked rapidly, trying to force his eyes to adjust. He saw a hump of darker white a few feet away. He crawled toward it.

His vision slowly cleared, and he saw that it was Max lying in front of him. Michael reached out and felt for Max's pulse. He could feel it, faint and erratic, but there.

"What did you do?" Trevor yelled.

Michael leaped to his feet and spun to face his brother. Trevor was staring down at the Stone. It lay dull and lifeless in his hand.

"What did you do to the Stone?" Trevor shouted, advancing on Max.

"I didn't do anything," Max answered as he struggled to sit up.

"I sure as hell didn't," Michael said.

"Oh, I guess it must have been me," Kyle announced from the doorway. Michael saw Adam, Alex, Isabel, Liz, and Maria trying to push their way past him.

"This little baby is fine." Kyle lovingly ran his fingers over the curved surface of the small silver disk in his hand.

Then he raised his eyes to Michael. "Now, you *will* tell me what I want to know."

# ROSWELL
## HIGH

## SOME SECRETS ARE TOO DANGEROUS TO KNOW. . .

### Don't miss Roswell High #9
# The Dark One

**Isabel** has run away from home, and Max knows her life is in danger. He has to find her and save her, but time is ticking away.

**Alex** is back on Earth, and he's a changed man. He looks better, feels better, and is ready to live life to the fullest—without Isabel Evans.  Little does he know he's the only person that can help the ailing Isabel. Will Alex be able to put aside his pride and save the life of his former love?

### Look out for Roswell High #10
# The Salvation
### Coming soon from Pocket Books!

# F E A R L E S S™

## ...a girl born without the fear gene

Seventeen-year-old Gaia Moore is not your typical high school senior. She is a black belt in karate, was doing advanced maths in junior school and, oh yes, she absolutely Does Not Care. About anything. Her mother is dead and her father, a covert anti-terrorist agent, abandoned her years ago. But before he did, he taught her self-preservation. Tom Moore knew there would be a lot of people after Gaia because of who, and what, she is. Gaia is genetically enhanced not to feel fear and her life has suddenly become dangerous. Her world is about to explode with terrorists, government spies and psychos bent on taking her apart. But Gaia does not care. She is Fearless.